The Amber Torch

The Altered Elite Series

Book 1

D. Burgard

The Amber Torch

Paperback ISBN: 978-0-9857582-6-4
Ebook ISBN: 978-0-9857582-3-3

Contents

*For the Burgard Boys,
one thru four*

The Altered Elite Series

—

The Amber Torch
Book 1

Joined in Fire
Book 2

The Imminent Storm
Book 3

Book 4 coming soon!

dburgardbooks.com

The Amber Torch

1

Gasping, I sit up, startling myself awake.

Not again.

My heart feels as though it's beating so hard it could beat right through my chest. Where are those damn shoes? I'm so hot I can barely stand it. I have to get out of here.

My eyes catch sight of the shoes right by the door, exactly where I always leave them. Frustrated, I grab them, slam my feet in, and with shaking fingers lace them up. Once my feet are cradled into that familiar feel, I open the window and am out without another thought.

***

I run. I run for minutes, hours, who knows. The streetlights cast an eerie glow as I pass the houses of my slumbering neighbors. The cold, dry desert air fills my lungs. Finally I feel my heart rate begin to slow, although my pace doesn't. Feeling my breathing getting steadier, I run like this for another minute. Regaining my own claim on a drained body, I slow then and finally begin to walk. My mind starts to clear as logic begins creeping itself back in.

I sit down on the curb, trying to wrap my head around the fact that it happened again. I lie back and feel the cool grass against my hot skin. My heart slows into a steady rhythmic pattern. I take a deep breath, and it comes out in shaky spurts. It feels good just to lie here so still and quiet, everything that I wasn't five minutes ago. I would love to give in to this calm feeling and just go to sleep right here, but as my body starts to fade, the noises of the night bring me back to reality. My nerves are jolted as I look around. Here I am outside in the middle of the night, lying on someone's lawn.

Standing up, I try to regain my composure, but my legs feel like they're going to give out underneath me. I start the slow tread back down the street in the direction of my house. I push away the usual uneasy feelings as I wonder how far I've run this time. A familiar cluster of palms adorns a certain cream-colored two-story adobe house. This is the house my eyes are drawn to every day as I come and go from the neighborhood. Although easy enough to pass by in the car, it's much too far to run to from my house.

I hate this part. The dreaded walk back.

It's been happening more often lately. The first time was a couple of months ago, and since then, I've definitely noticed a trend. I can usually count on an especially bad day at school to trigger it. Like the day Mr. Hutchins decided I was going to be his object of ridicule in my public speaking class.

Glancing around anxiously, I turn the corner and see the floodlight is on. My spirits are immediately lifted. If Mark's out playing, it means he must have had a rough night, too. I would know about that.

He's the boy I've wanted for as long as I can remember. We've both lived in this neighborhood since we were little kids, riding bikes, playing ball. All the things you do with your neighborhood friends until you discover the boys have more to offer than just being best at kickball. Once you figure that out, it's time to go your separate ways.

As I get closer to his house, I duck behind the big cottonwood tree in Mr. Bentley's yard and sit. The huge tree helps block me from view. How many nights lately have I sat here after a run and watched him play? His motions are fluid, and he makes a basket without even trying. Perfection. He dribbles the ball as if it were an extension of himself. Tonight there is an edge to his movements, like a smoldering anger beneath his usual grace. The rim makes a loud bang as he flies through the air and slams the ball in.

The whole town knows his story. The dad that skipped out when he was a kid. The alcoholic mom that seems to live in her own world most of the time. How he has to raise his younger brother and take care of himself. Although his family life is anything but stellar, he's the best basketball player at my high school. In this town that's everything.

I'm happy that he's out tonight. Watching him play takes my mind off things.

He stops playing then and throws the ball into the fence with such a force there's a loud smack. He seems really upset and I suppress the urge to run to him. I guess appearing out of the shadows right now might come across as a little odd.

Instead I just sit here and watch him turn off the light and go in. I'm thankful I just live right down the street. Feeling the cold air and stiffness in my legs only makes me want to be home in my bed. Its blankets wrapping me in its comforting warm embrace.

My cell phone alarm goes off, and it takes me a minute to realize what's happening. My whole body is sore. I stretch and try to loosen up a bit. Standing up, a wave of nausea comes over me so I close my eyes and take a deep breath. It passes after a couple of seconds but I know it will come again. This happens every morning after an episode.

I go into the bathroom and splash water on my face and brush my teeth. That perks me up a little. My hair is long and brown. Not the rich chestnut brown or the trendy mocha or some other popular coffee-name brown, no, it's just a light brown. As I run a brush through it a few times I appreciate the fact that, although it has a rather uninteresting color, it's relatively low maintenance. Even if it weren't, washing it every couple of days and occasionally brushing it is about all I can stand. I just don't have the patience or skill to do much else. I throw on a little makeup and get dressed. Jeans and a simple short-sleeved shirt. It's blue with a scoop neck. Standard fare for me. I put on my favorite silver small-hoop earrings. The ones my parents got me two years ago for my birthday. There are a couple of small diamonds on each one. That's about as much bling as I can stand.

I run downstairs, looking for my brown shoes, the clunky ones I wear almost every day.

As usual my dad's already at school to teach an early class. It's one of the large universities here and he's built quite a reputation for himself. He's been working there for so long, he could teach in his sleep. That was, before he started working on the grant. Now his research keeps him continuously preoccupied. Something to do with extraterrestrial mineralogy. Yeah, he's a geeky sci-fi professor.

My mom's out of town again this week. It's kind of the story of her career life. When she's in town she works from home, but traveling is something of a necessity in her line of work: money. She works in finance for some large corporation housed in many areas around the country. One being here, in the state of perpetual sunshine—her words actually. After having to visit cold, wetter climates all the time, she's always happy to be back. Warm and dry.

Before I came along my parents lived for their jobs, but

once they adopted me things were different, or so they say. I find it hard to believe that two people could possibly work harder than they do, but honestly, I like my alone time so it works as far as I'm concerned.

I spot my shoes in the kitchen under the table and realize then that my dad must have moved them there. On top of the table is a blueberry muffin and glass of milk. I haven't been totally forgotten.

I love mornings like this. I don't have to interact with anyone while I get ready. It gives me a chance to get my thoughts in order before school and all the social ramifications associated with it. I put on my shoes and grab my backpack just as I hear the honk from outside. Right on time as usual.

I walk outside and see Julian's car. I look down the street toward Mark's house. Hope he's having a better day today. I walk up to the car and climb in the back.

There to greet me with a "Hey you" is Aiden. He's blondish with hazel eyes. He's been a part of my life, basically my best friend, for years.

Julian, the one who drives our little trio around, shoots me a big grin. He became my other best friend when he moved here at the beginning of the last school year. Aiden and I got to know him from the track team, and before we knew it the three of us were hanging out all the time.

"You look tired. Rough night?" Julian says, looking at me with an odd expression. He's got dark brown hair and blue eyes. Piercing eyes. The kind of eyes that never miss a thing. The kind of eyes that every girl in the school can't get enough of, and he knows it.

I shrug dismissively.

"I guess I had too much caffeine before bed."

"Oh. . . right," he says giving me one of those you're-full-of-shit looks.

Aiden chimes in then. "Julian was just filling me in on

some of his weekend exploits. Why don't you tell Jo about Taylor and her friend Ashley from—"

"No thank you, I'll pass," I say, holding up my hand hoping not to hear another word about Julian and his recent conquest.

They both start laughing. Although it seems as though Julian has been with most of the girls in the school, he's never seemed to like any of them. Not for more than a few nights anyway. I sometimes wonder how much of what he says is true or if Julian just says things to get a rise out of me. Come to think of it, knowing Julian, it's probably all true.

At school, I stand at my locker blankly staring at the books inside. My real attention is on the couple down the hall. I can hear her murmuring something to him in that low voice that's almost like a purr. Their displays would be rather entertaining if they didn't get under my skin so much. She squeals and throws her arms around him before kissing him on the cheek and strutting away down the hall. Watching her leave, I wonder how exactly he's able to put up with her.

Sahara is captain of the cheerleading squad. Perky, blond, and popular. She knows it. If her looks were any reflection of her personality, she would be grotesque. She started here at the beginning of last year and once she saw Mark, she seemed determined to claim him as her own.

Walking into the lunchroom I head straight for our usual table. I can tell as I approach that Julian and Aiden are in some sort of heavy discussion. Julian has a pensive look on his face and Aiden seems deep in thought.

"Hey," I say as I put my backpack on the table and pull

a bag of chips, an apple, and a Coke out. Julian looks up and says, "Hey."

"What's going on?" I say as I bite into the apple. My eyes water from its tartness. They both look at me, and Aiden shoves the city's number-one source for news, as they say, at me. The Tribune. There on page three is a picture of a very pretty dark-haired girl. I look up at Aiden.

"Yeah I know, it's happened again."

Over the course of the last six months, our city has had a string of unexplained deaths and a whole crop of missing person cases come up. When it all started they were finding a body every couple of days. Men and women of all different cultures and backgrounds. There didn't seem to be any reason to it. Then the killings all but stopped a couple of months ago, only to start back up just recently. I think back on my nightly runs. A chill runs through me thinking of myself out there alone, vulnerable. Of course when I'm in the thick of it, I'm not thinking too clearly.

"This is the third person this month," I say, unable to take my eyes off the girl's face.

It's weird to think that just yesterday this girl was probably sitting in her own cafeteria with her friends. Thinking about schoolwork, activities, boys . . . who knows. Now she's gone. Did she know she was going to die? Did she suffer? I stop reading when it gets to some graphic explanation of how she was found.

"It said that it looked to be the same cause of death as the others," Aiden says. "Not only had her torso been burned from the inside, even her clothes were singed."

"On that note, I gotta run to class," I say and give them a weak smile as I grab my backpack and sling it over my shoulder. "See you at track."

I laugh as I watch Julian give Coach Miller a hard time about his drill times. Although Julian is the best runner on the boys' team, he rarely takes it seriously. He spends most of his time kidding around or messing with Aiden, which drives Aiden crazy.

I'm amazed watching Julian run. How effortless it is for him as he flies around the track. I myself have always been an average runner. It's really the story of my life. I've always been average at just about everything. Of course that was before I started having these episodes. Now I find I can do things I wasn't able to before. Like when our gym teacher had everyone practice their archery skills. Usually this would be a joke for me, but on this particular day things were different. I couldn't miss. I mean, I really couldn't miss. The archery team "Bull's-eye" has been hot to recruit me ever since.

When practice finally ends, I see Julian and Aiden heading my way.

"Did I tell you guys about my plans for the talent show?" Julian asks, giving me a wink.

"Only a hundred times, man, give it a rest," Aiden says, looking exasperated.

Laughing at them, I turn to Julian.

"I still think you should go the serious route this year. I mean, wow, if they heard you play—"

"Oh, no way. These people wouldn't recognize real talent. Besides, it would mess with my rep. I don't think chicks really dig the concert pianist type."

"You'd be surprised, Julian. Not every girl in this school thinks like your friends Taylor and what's-her-face."

"Maybe so, but it's the way they think that I like," he says smiling and raising his eyebrows at me.

"You're gross, you know that."

"I believe they'd beg to differ," he says laughing.

After track practice, Aiden and I go over to Julian's to listen to his new composition. He's the most talented pianist I've ever heard. Not that I know what I'm hearing since I'm exceptionally musically challenged. Let's just say when it came to picking an instrument in sixth grade, the teacher finally gave up on me and assigned me to help percussion with the cymbal.

We walk into his music studio, and Aiden and I sit down on my favorite red velvety couch. I run my hand along its softness and look around the room. We've been here so many times, yet I still can't get used to the wealth. Julian comes from money. Even so, if it weren't for that ridiculously expensive car of his, I don't think anyone would even know. He doesn't have a pretentious bone in his body.

Julian begins to play and I'm spellbound. As I sit there, I can feel my emotions start to stir. The melody is beautiful. Julian's lean frame slightly bent over the keys. His perfectly flawless skin contrasts with his dark, wavy hair. His hair is thick and has a silky sheen to it. His fingers move in such a way it's as if he's massaging the keys. His intensity is mesmerizing. This is the side of Julian we see only when he's playing.

I look over at Aiden and catch him watching me. It's as if he was reading my mind, and I blush slightly. He gives me a slight smile and looks away. All of a sudden I'm feeling uncomfortable. I don't know if it's the music or what. Aiden and I lock eyes, and I see what I've known for quite some time. He has feelings for me. I guess it's something I've known for awhile, but when it's your best friend, it's easier to ignore the signs rather than just make things weird. Besides, he and Julian know how crazy I am for Mark. They make fun of me all the time about it.

I pull my eyes away from his just as I feel his hand touch mine. His touch is hot, and I feel a galvanic response to it. I wonder what that means? I don't pull my hand away until Julian finishes the song, and then I start clapping. Relieved that whatever this thing was that was happening is over. I ignore Aiden the rest of the afternoon.

I get to our usual lunchroom table first the next day. As I sit there my eyes are on Sahara and her entourage. She flits around the table from one person to the next. Does that girl ever just stop and chill? Watching her makes me exhausted.

Mark's sitting there just staring out. I can tell by the look on his face he's either tired or has a lot on his mind. Was he out playing basketball last night? Although I'm glad I didn't have an episode, part of me feels like I missed out on an opportunity.

How can Sahara not even notice that something's wrong? How can she be that out of tune to someone's feelings? Oh man, what I would do to trade places with her even for just one day.

Mark looks up and catches my stare. I'm unable to look away, and he gives me a curious smile. Aiden walks up and sits down, and I can tell right away he's still acting weird. On the car ride this morning, he barely said a word. Julian was rambling on and on about some science experiment gone bad in Mr. Woods's class yesterday. The story was kind of amusing, but it was hard not to notice Aiden just sitting there stewing.

Aiden's been a constant in my life since I can remember. Someone I could count on. When my dog died in fifth grade, he was there with me and my parents at our backyard funeral. He even had a few kind words to say about old Puddles.

He's always been my only really good friend. That person you can always count on, always there for you. We hung out almost everyday. We'd play board games at my house, which I loved and I know he hated. We'd ride our bikes around the neighborhood every day. We even started a club in his backyard. We took over his little sister's playhouse and only allowed certain kids to take part. Of course one of them was his sister since we would have gotten in trouble with his mom for not letting her in her own playhouse. We didn't have too many kids in our club, and the ones we did have were younger and thought we were cool. Honestly, I really think we just enjoyed having something that was ours. An excuse to hang out.

Even when we were in middle school and I started liking Mark and he started hanging out with Ray and his group of annoying jocks did we not keep our friendship going.

I couldn't imagine not having him in my life.

"How's your day going?" I say to him, hoping to break this funk we're in. He gives me a look like I know what you're trying to do.

"It's going."

I glance over at Mark's table, but he's gone. Sahara's still there with a few girls from the cheerleading squad. She gives me a weird look.

"Hey freaks, any big plans this weekend?" Julian says and sits down next to me. He has a tray piled high with food. How can he eat so much? Seeing all that food makes my stomach turn. I must be coming down with something because I haven't been feeling right since my last episode.

"I've got a paper to work on for my creative writing class," I say. I dread it. What takes a normal person a couple of hours to write can take me a day. Not a creative bone in my body.

"Yeah, I'm slammed," Aiden says in a less-than-excited tone.

Just then Sahara and two girls saunter up to the table. Looking only at Aiden as if we aren't there, she says, "Hey Aiden, you going to Zac's party tonight?"

He just looks at her in a confused way.

"Carissa was just telling me how she would love it if you were there."

I look over at the girl named Carissa standing slightly behind her. She has a knowing smile on her face, and her eyes are locked onto Aiden. I'm shocked that these girls are not only standing here but are inviting him to a party. What exactly do they want with him? They seem like two cobras charming their prey before they strike. I can feel myself getting protective of my friend, and my temperature rises. I shift in my seat uncomfortably, and Sahara looks at me briefly then puts her eyes right back on Aiden.

"Um, I don't know," he says and gives the girl Carissa a baffled look. Sahara smiles at him and leans over to whisper in his ear in a seductive voice, "Well . . . if you come, I just know you'll have a good time."

She straightens up and adds in a perky tone before walking off, "See you tonight," and flashes him a huge smile. He stares after them until they've all walked out of the lunchroom.

"What was that?" Julian says, bringing his attention back to us. Aiden looks at me and his stupid little grin turns to concern. "Jo, you all right?"

At that moment I'm feeling really hot and agitated. I want to jump up, run after Sahara and her friends, and wipe those smug little looks off their faces. Why am I feeling like this? What's wrong with me?

Aiden reaches out and touches my hand. "You're hot!" he says looking at my hand with a strange expression on his face.

I yank my arm away and fold my hands on my lap.

"I must be coming down with something. I'm gonna go get some air." And I jump up from the table, grab my backpack, and head outside, leaving Aiden and Julian staring after me.

The cool air instantly makes me feel better. It hasn't started getting hot yet, and I'm thankful for that. Pacing around a bit, I breathe in slowly, trying to get a handle on my thoughts, but my mind's racing.

I already have issues with Sahara and her annoying attachment to Mark, but to start slinking around Aiden is completely unacceptable. Julian and even Mark can take care of themselves around her type, but Aiden. . .

I sit down at one of the picnic tables and take a book out of my bag. I have no intention of reading it but want to look busy. I just need a moment to myself to sort out my thoughts.

Why am I feeling so protective of Aiden? He's my best friend, and I know we're going through a weird patch in our relationship right now, but why do I feel threatened?

Ugh. . . I'm so confused, and it doesn't help when my body starts kicking into overdrive every time I start to feel like this. Annoyed and slightly embarrassed with myself, I just sit at the picnic table for a while pretending to read my book.

Starting to get a handle on my thoughts, I wonder what really set me off. I know I don't like that Sahara girl, and the party invite was weird, but honestly it wasn't that big of a deal. Why would it cause me to start my craziness? I just sit here breathing in and out. Focusing on getting a complete sense of control.

I realize now I was beginning to have one of my episodes back there. It's bad enough when it happens at night. . . How am I going to deal with this? I can't keep acting like I'm coming down with the flu.

Just sitting out here in the cool breeze calms me and helps to clear my head. Maybe I'm just going through teen-age hormone stuff. Seems a little extreme, but possible I guess. I chalk it up to that for now and go inside.

2

—

That afternoon I rush out to the track before everyone else just to warm up a bit. I want to make sure when I start running, it won't set me off or something. I notice Julian and Aiden coming out with a group of boys. Julian shoots me a huge grin, but Aiden barely looks at me. For the rest of practice I'm mediocre at best.

At the end of practice I walk toward Aiden, feeling unsure about what to say but knowing that I have to say something. I have to make things right. This thing between us is weird and terrible. As I get closer, I find my courage fleeting. I've never been good with emotional conversations, having always shied away from expressing my feelings. Anything that even remotely seems dramatic and I'm a no-go.

"Hey," I say, falling in step with him as he walks around the track.

"Hey Jo," he says back not looking my way. We walk like that for a few minutes until Julian runs up behind us.

"So you never answered me, you going to that party tonight?"

"No, I don't know those people. It would be weird," Aiden says. "Honestly, I really don't know why they invited me."

"Because that Carissa chick must like you," Julian says and gives him a smile, lifting his eyebrows.

Aiden then glances at me and we lock eyes for a second. Looking ahead I say, "She's a cute girl. You could have a fun night."

Julian chimes in enthusiastically, "Jo and I could go with you as backup in case you get in over your head."

Aiden shoots him an angry look and says, "I'm not an idiot, I think I can handle myself."

"Oh yeah? Like you did when I beat your ass earlier on that drill?" Julian taunts. That seems to rub Aiden the wrong way. I can tell he's getting mad.

"Don't listen to him, he's just trying to get you to take him to that stupid party," I say and reach out to touch his arm. He's hot, I mean really hot. He yanks his arm away and looks at Julian, "Ok bitch, lets do this!

Two laps?" Julian asks. Aiden nods and they're off.

I just stand there watching them race each other. Julian is a better runner, but Aiden seems determined. As they come around the bend on the second lap, they're neck and neck, but I can tell Julian is holding back . . . toying with him. What I don't understand, though, is why? Just then Julian glances my way and takes off with a burst of speed that seems unnatural. How could he have held back so much? Baffled, I watch as he leaves Aiden in the dust and then runs right past me, just to twist the knife in. I look back at Aiden, and he's stopped running just a few feet away from me. He turns to walk off the track, and I jog to catch up.

After I catch up with him, we walk silently side by side. What can I say to make this whole situation better?

"Don't worry about it. Julian's just being a jerk."

He just keeps walking at a fast pace, ignoring me as I try my hardest to keep up next to him.

Just then he stops walking, grabs my arm, and swings me around to face him. He looks so flustered, so agitated. Even his eyes have a different look to them. I notice again how hot his touch is. Burning.

"Jo . . . you know how I feel about you. I want us to be more than friends."

He's looking at me so intensely that I can't breathe. I don't utter a sound. I can't. What do I say? How do I feel about him? All I can do is stand there and look at him blankly.

We stand like that for what seems like eternity, and then his face changes and he says in a calm voice, "Well, there you have it Jo—sorry to make you feel uncomfortable." Then he walks away.

I just stand there watching him.

On the ride home I'm quiet. Julian has the radio turned up louder than normal and I'm glad. I steal glances at Aiden as he sits in the passenger seat of Julian's car just staring out the window. He's my best friend. What happens now? How do I get things back to the way they used to be when everything was so simple?

Later when I get home, I go upstairs and jump in the shower. I'm washing away not only the sweat from practice but the weirdness of the day. I stay in the shower longer than normal but am feeling better when I get out. Wrapped in my towel, I lie on my bed for a while. Aiden was hot to the touch. Really hot. That's one of the symptoms of my episodes. Could he have the same problem I do? Could it be something that we've both caught?

I go over to my computer. I search for information about some of the symptoms I've been having. Nothing. Nothing that ties everything together. It doesn't make sense.

What about Aiden? Is that why he looked at me so strangely in the lunchroom after touching my hand? Is he going through the same thing?

All of a sudden I push all the strange feelings aside. All

I want to do is protect him. Protect my friend. I pick up my phone and call Julian.

I hear his car pull up. My mom came back into town last night, so my parents are having a few friends over tonight. I'm glad I won't have to sit here making up things about my future goals and ambitions. Adults love to know what your life plans are. But since I don't really have any—I mean, I am planning to go to college and all, I already have my golden ticket to get in. Since my dad's been with the university forever, he has tons of strings to pull.

While most kids can rattle off their life's dreams and ambitions, it's the after college plans that have always been hazy to me. I used to think it was because I was adopted. That maybe my biological parents were bums and some of those underachiever genes are floating around inside me. But now, with all these strange things happening to me. . .

I say good-bye to my dad and am reminded of the time I'm expected back. This makes me smile. I hardly ever do anything socially, and if I do, I'm always back way before most kids my age are even finished getting ready to go out. I'm happy that my dad gets to play "the strict father with a teenage daughter" role for once. Gives him a little taste of what his friends with teenage kids must complain about.

Julian is sitting in the car on the phone when I get in. He hangs up and looks at me with an odd expression. Not his usual big grin.

"So Jo, ready to part-ay?"

"I guess so," I say.

"I was surprised you called wanting to go tonight."

"I know. I guess I figure we're sending Aiden to the wolves and all. Besides, I don't know, I don't like that Carissa girl, and why is she all of a sudden interested? I mean, we've been in school for how many months already this year with not so much as a glance his way, and now she really wants him to hang out with her. It's just weird if you ask me. I figure we'll show up and at least have his back if she ends up turning into a teenage mutant vampire or something."

This makes Julian smile and he says, "Now this party is starting to sound a lot more interesting."

We pull up to the house. It's a huge two-story house with a long balcony upstairs overlooking the driveway. It looks rather out of place with its many stones. Not the typical kind of house that's around this area of the Southwest. Even the landscape, with its lush green trees, is unlike most of the yards here with their interesting mix of palms, cacti, and broad-leafed plants. Everything that's unique and unequaled about a desert landscape.

I suddenly feel like I'm walking up to one of the houses you would see on the cover of a home-and-garden magazine. The one where there's always pumpkins and sunflowers all around in the fall.

I recognize a couple of the football players from school hanging out on the front porch. Whatever they are talking about must be very interesting because they don't even look our way as Julian and I climb the steps.

We go up to the door, which is already ajar. I can hear loud music booming from inside. With the music and strange surroundings, I feel suddenly very out of place. I can't imagine that Aiden is actually in there. My mind switches over to Mark. From what I know, Mark hangs out with everyone at school but rarely participates in much away from school other than the occasional victory party after a basketball game. I wonder if he will be here tonight, though. Just the thought of seeing him gives me a new sense of excitement.

I push the door open, and Julian and I go inside. There are kids everywhere. Some dancing, some sitting. Most just standing around. A lot of red plastic cups.

We walk through a huge living room. Wood walls with wood trimming. Stones interlaced throughout. All I can think of is ski lodge.

Then I see him. Aiden is sitting on a sofa in the back of the room looking disinterested as Carissa and some other girls are around him talking. He takes an occasional drink from a red cup.

Julian and I exchange looks, and then Julian heads straight up to him with me following and wishing now that I hadn't come. Whatever is wrong between Aiden and I can surely wait until Monday.

"Yo, party animal," Julian says to Aiden. He looks up at Julian and then toward me. "What are you guys doing here?"

Then Sahara is there. "Exactly. What are you guys doing here?" she says and gives Julian a look.

Julian ignores her. Her comment bothers him, and she seems to know it. Trying to change the mood, I ask without even thinking, "Mark here with you tonight?"

Aiden, Julian, and Sahara all look at me. The expression on their faces says a lot. This whole night is shaping up to be a huge mistake.

In the most monotone voice I've ever heard, Sahara says, "Mark isn't here. He had to do something with his brother. I guess his mom is on another one of her benders. . . Sorry Jo." Then she turns and walks off, leaving me feeling like the biggest idiot.

Carissa leans over and whispers something in Aiden's ear. I suddenly remember why I'm even here at all tonight. Completely ignoring Carissa, I say to Aiden, "Can I talk to you outside for a moment?"

I can tell the Mark comment is still stewing around in his head. He looks at me with a mixture of hurt and anger and says, "Carissa and I were on our way somewhere." He stands up takes her arm and leads her away, only pausing for a moment to turn and give me one final look.

Part of me wants to run and stop him. To insist that he listen to what I have to say about the weird things that have been happening. That is why I'm here . . . right?

But nothing comes out. As I watch he and Carissa disappear down a dark hall.

I turn around and find Julian watching the exchange with unwavering intensity. I look up at him and say, "Lets go."

It takes him a moment to focus on what I'm saying, but I'm not hanging around waiting for his mind to play catch up. I bump into people as I weave my way out. The room seems much more crowded than before. I finally get through and step onto the front porch.

Fresh air. I realize now how stuffy it was in there. I'm feeling very hot, and a part of me starts to panic slightly. It's nothing. I'm just feeling hot from being enclosed with so many people. Being outside is already making me feel much cooler.

I walk toward Julian's car but then turn around to wait for him. He's right behind me. He's mad. I give him a puzzled look, as he walks past me and up to his car. He unlocks the doors with his remote and then gets in the driver's side. I climb in next to him, shut my door, and wonder if I missed something.

" Look, if you don't want to leave I—"

"You and Aiden. . . is something going on?" Julian asks angrily. "You guys have both been acting weird lately. Whenever I'm around, you both clam up or give each other looks. I feel like I'm your lackey. I'm here whenever you need me, but I don't know what's going on inside that head of yours. When did the rules change? When did you decide that Aiden was allowed in?"

He's right. I've always been a closed-off person. I've never allowed anyone to really get close to me.

I think about the episodes I've been having. How this connection with Aiden caused me to want to come here tonight. I mean this is the only reason I am here, right? Regardless, I would never want to make Julian feel excluded or hurt in any way. What do I say to him? I can't talk about my episodes with him. I won't.

"I know this all seems strange and you're right, we have been acting weird lately but. . . " What else can I say? How do I explain? I just sit there trying to find the right words to say.

Julian just looks like he's waiting for more of an explanation. When I say nothing, he starts the engine, and drives off.

We ride in silence until we get to my house. In the driveway, he just sits there looking straight ahead. What can I say? I need to say something. I can't have them both mad at me.

But I have nothing. I just stare at his profile for a minute, open the door, and get out.

When I close the door, he takes off. I hear his tires squeal as he makes the turn off my street.

What a disaster.

I sigh and look toward my house. I'm back way before my curfew. My parents' friends are still there. As I'm in no mood for conversation, I decide to just go for a walk. It'll give me a chance to be numb for a little while.

I head down the road in the direction of Mark's house. Sitting there watching him play would be comforting. I really need that right now.

As I turn the corner, I see the lights are off. I'm disappointed but somewhat relieved that maybe things turned out all right with his mom tonight.

I just keep walking.

All these thoughts and feelings are swirling around in my head. I'm not sure what to think anymore. Aiden and Julian. Everything's all messed up, and whatever I try to do or say just seems to make things worse.

Ugh. I really just want things to go back to the way they were.

"Hi Jo, what are you doing out here?" I hear a male voice ask, breaking me out of my trance.

Focusing, I realize I'm standing in the street right in front of Mark's house just staring. What the hell am I doing? I must look like the biggest freak ever. My first instinct is to turn and run, or maybe I'll just wake up and realize I've just been in a bad dream. A really bad dream.

No such luck.

I am actually standing here, at night, in the middle of the street, in front of the house of the one boy on earth that I wouldn't want to do anything strange in front of.

He's staring at me as if he's waiting for me to explain myself. What do I say? Oh hey, Mark, don't mind me, I'm just staring at your house like a psycho.

I just stand there looking into those beautiful brown eyes. The same brown eyes that have repeatedly graced my dreams over again. The eyes that I'll catch a glimpse of as he passes me in the hall at school or that I've connected with on those few occasions that I think about all the time.

"Uh . . . Jo, you all right?" he asks.

I snap back. My mind focuses again on my surroundings and where I am.

I smile then. A huge smile that says I'm sure of myself and well aware of my actions. If there's one thing I've learned from watching Sahara and her obnoxious ways, it's how to react to things in such a way that nobody would ever doubt that she doesn't know exactly what she's doing. She sells it. Now I'm trying to.

"Oh hey, Mark," I say still holding onto that smile. "My parents have a few friends over so I thought I'd stay out of their hair and go for a walk. I thought I heard something by your house, but it was actually you. I guess you just startled me." I let out a small laugh.

"Yeah, I was just gonna come out and shoot some hoops when I saw your shadow. I guess we scared each other a bit," he says, smiling back at me.

I don't know if it is wishful thinking on my part or what, but a part of me picks up on the fact that he seems happy to see me. Just the thought of it gets my heart racing.

He looks back toward his house then and says, "I wouldn't mind taking a walk myself. Can I tag along?"

Is he kidding? "Sure, I guess it's better that I'm not alone anyway, huh," I say, suddenly feeling very wary of where I am. "Yeah, you're right, there have been some terrible things happening lately."

We walk in silence for a minute. I think about that girl with the dark hair. I see her face looking back at me and all my problems seem meaningless. There's something bigger going on in this town, and if I don't get my head straight. . .

I look over at Mark and catch him staring at me. He gives me a weak smile then looks straight ahead and asks, "You have any track meets coming up?"

He's probably trying to keep the conversation light because I seem out of sorts tonight. "We do have one coming up sometime soon," I say, feigning enthusiasm. "I usually enjoy practice, but I get a little nervous before the meets."

He laughs slightly then and adds, "I know what you're saying. I get the same way before a game. They say it's a good thing, though. You'll perform better."

"They say that, huh? I haven't had the pleasure of that one actually working for me yet," I say. We both laugh.

We talk about school, certain teachers, the latest gossip.

The conversation is effortless. He is so easy to talk to. We laugh a lot.

He walks me home and I'm happy. Happy to see the visitors are gone. Happy that I'm with him. Just happy. Giddy almost. This night was a roller coaster, but now I'm glad I got on the ride. Very glad.

We say goodnight without any of the awkwardness like you see in the movies.

After saying goodnight to my parents, hearing about their evening and all the exploits of Dr. Mills and his wife, I go up to my room. I'm on cloud nine. I think about Aiden and Julian and all the work I'm going to have to do on Monday, but for now I'm happy. Nothing I think about can wipe the grin off my face. Nothing could make me feel bad.

3

When I wake up, it's late. The sun is shining through my curtains with the strength of midday.

It's Saturday. My mom was going to be flying out early this morning. Something to do with a crisis at one of the Washington hubs. I'm sure dad's at the university. With all the work needed to be done on the research grant, he's been going in a lot more lately. Also, since they are working with actual test subjects now, Saturdays are his busy days.

I stretch and my head feels heavy. I slept like a rock. It's been a long time since I've done that. I just lie there for a while going through the events of the night before. I dread having to deal with Aiden and Julian, but the promise of things to come with Mark gives me a sense of excitement.

After showering I go downstairs but I have no appetite at all. I have butterflies in my stomach, and all I can think about is Mark.

I hear a car pull up. That's strange. I practically skip to the window and look out to see Julian's car out front. Watching him get out, I wonder what he's doing here. Probably came to talk about how we left things last night. I'm too happy to be upset with him anyway. All I want is to have my friend back so I can tell him what happened after he dropped me off. I go over to the door, pause when I see his face through the glass. He's just standing there looking down. Almost as if he's trying to get the courage to knock. He looks miserable. I suddenly feel guilty for being happy at all. Obviously our spat bothered him more than I thought.

I swing the door open and just want to throw my arms around him to make him feel better, but stop when he looks up. Our eyes lock, and I'm confused by what I see.

What's that look he's giving me? I'm trying to read him but I can't. We just stand there looking at each other. After what seems like forever, he just grabs me and hugs me tight.

"Aiden was killed last night."

My mind tries to grasp what Julian just said to me, but it's incomprehensible.

I can barely breathe.

"It was like the other murders," he whispers.

This can't be happening. It just can't be. Not to Aiden. Not to him. Not to my best friend. I'm sobbing now. I'm holding onto Julian and sobbing.

Julian holds me for as long as I need him. I pull away and look at him. I can tell he wants to shield me from this misery, from all my sadness.

I turn and get only as far as the living room before my body stops. I can't move . . . can't speak. All I can do is stand there and stare. My mind is a whirlwind. I'm seeing Aiden as a boy in our clubhouse explaining to some little kid what he'll have to do to come in. He's there smiling at me as I try to get my dad's car into the right gear but grind the clutch mercilessly. Giving me words of encouragement at our last track meet.

"He can't be gone. How can he be gone? What will I do?" I'm crying again now. Uncontrollable sobs. My eyes and nose are burning. My whole body is shaking. Julian is there, his strength matching my weakness. At this point he's holding me up.

The front door opens and I see my dad come through. He knows. He is heading for me now. His baby girl needs him, and the pain on his face makes my sorrow all the worse. I throw myself into his arms as the sobs keep coming.

✳

On Sunday, I lie awake feeling numb and exhausted. I'm not sure how long I've been just lying here when my dad comes in my room.

He tentatively walks in and sits on the edge of my bed.

"How are you doing, Josie?"

My name is Josephine yet nobody calls me that. It's either Jo or Josie. That's just the way things have been for as long as I can remember, but the thing is, I actually like the name Josephine.

Sitting up, I look at him. "Better I guess," I say, although I don't recognize my voice. It's hoarse and raspy. Giving me a concerned look he says, "Your mom wants me to make sure you eat something. What sounds good?"

I smile then. I can imagine my mom saying that. That's always been our thing. Her constant need to feed me and my resistance to it. My thin frame is a constant reminder of her need to get me to eat something. To nurture me. Honestly, it's the only way she does.

"Whatever is fine," I say knowing he'll be relieved. He smiles then.

"Your mom's headed back early. She should be home sometime tonight."

I feel bad all of a sudden. Her leaving early will cause all kinds of problems for her at work.

"She doesn't have to do that. Really dad, I'm fine. Call her and tell her to just stay there and take care of the problem," I say, giving him a big smile, hoping to convince him. Honestly, the thought of my mom feeling the obligation to be here in hover mode is enough to send me back into a depressive state.

My dad gives me that look that tells me he's not so sure.

"Well, ok. . . I'll get you something to eat and call her. I might not be able to catch her before she leaves, though," he says and pats my leg then walks out.

I fall back into the bed, thinking how ironic it is that any time a kid needs a little more reassurance from their parents, they usually end up having to reassure them.

My head is killing me. I close my eyes hoping to relieve the throbbing but Aiden's face pops into my mind. Now I feel something way worse. A hollowness in the pit of my stomach. I turn on my side, and the tears start to flow again as memories flood my thoughts.

I must have dozed off again. I look over and see a tray on my desk. On the tray is a sandwich, chips, and a Coke. My favorite. Realizing I'm starving, I dig in.

After eating I jump in the shower and feel a surge of energy. Aiden pops into my head, but I quickly push the thought away and focus on washing my hair. It's hard to keep my mind blank, so I fill it with the mundane tasks of everyday life. Much-needed distractions.

I get dressed and take my tray down to the kitchen. I don't hear anything, so I assume my mom is staying in Washington for the time being and my dad is probably in his office working on the grant. I peek around the corner and see him there. He's totally engrossed in his work as I stand there watching him. I'm always amazed at the speed at which he's able to type. The keys clicking with an uncanny speed without so much as a pause. I guess he gets plenty of practice, but still.

The office is one of the biggest rooms in our house. My

parents practically live there when they're home. On the opposite wall from the door is a large window with these incredibly plush window coverings. My mom has very ornate taste when it comes to interior design. Sitting in front of the window is my dad's huge mahogany desk with his computer facing the window. He always says how much he hates having doors to his back. Makes him on edge or something. Along the walls on either side of the desk are built-in shelves that house the hundreds of books that my parents own. The most being boring science books.

Looking up, he stops typing and seems relieved. I'm sure he's happy to see me up and showered. Showing signs of life.

"Did you get a hold of mom?" I say.

"Yep, I caught her and told her what you said. She was going to come anyway, but I convinced her that you were as you said . . . fine." Smiling that knowing smile of his he adds, "You owe me."

I laugh. I guess I'm always easy to read.

The house phone rings then and I just stand there unflinching. The last thing in the world I want right now is to talk to someone. Neither one of us makes a move to answer it.

"It's probably Julian again. He's been calling off and on to check on you ever since he left."

Aiden flashes in my mind again and my eyes well up. For a brief moment I think of Julian standing there looking down at me. I really need to call him and reassure him that I am fine. But I'm tinkering on the edge as it is.

The phone stops ringing. Silence again.

"I did tell him that you might not be going to school tomorrow," dad says, looking at me questioningly. "When I talked to him a few hours ago, I didn't think you'd be coming out of your room today. If you want to go, I can let him know when he calls again later."

School. School without Aiden. I think of going through

the typical motions of school and not having him there. Not only feeling, but living, with the huge void that is in my life now. Doing it around all those people. It's unthinkable.

"Yeah, I think I will stay home tomorrow." And at that moment I feel myself slipping back. Slipping back into the dark world of sadness. I can't say another word. I can't stand there anymore. I run upstairs and throw myself on the bed as the sobs work their way up from the hollow pit in my stomach. Will I ever feel right again? Should I?

When I wake up again, it dark outside. I get up and look at the clock on my computer, realizing it's the middle of the night. It's a little after 3 a.m. and I'm wide-awake, so I just sit down in my desk chair and stare at the computer monitor. I can't lie down any longer. My muscles are feeling sore from lack of use.

Sitting here, blankly staring at the screen, my mind seems settled, finally. Before I'm able to really think about what I'm doing, I bring up the website for our local news. The seven-day weather forecast is on the front page. Sun after sun.

I start scrolling down through the different articles until I get to the one I'm looking for. There smiling at me is his picture. It's the picture from last year's yearbook. I remember telling him I thought it was a good picture of him. For a yearbook picture, it had captured his natural smile. He flashed me that smile then, and I laughed as I said, "See, there it is."

To think this year's picture of him will be in that special place in the back of the yearbook. That place reserved for kids whose lives were cut short.

I stop and breathe. I start reading the words by the picture of my friend. My mind keeps drifting. Murdered. I'm having a hard time wrapping my head around it. I go back to the beginning of the article and start again. It's just like that pretty dark-haired girl, but this is different. She was someone I didn't know, could feel sorry for even, but this was Aiden. This couldn't have happened to him. How could it? These types of things don't happen to the people you care about.

I get to the part of the article that talks about where and how they found the body. The body. He was so much more than that. It's talking about a "clearing just down the road from a party he had attended to earlier that evening." The party. The party where I last saw him. Where I left on strange terms because I was too stupid to tell him how I feel. How I felt.

My mind starts wandering over the last few days. The days where I was irritated that he wanted to be more than friends. The days I was acting like anything but a friend. That's when it hits me. The feeling that is now sending me flying to my bed as the flood of emotions start again. The feelings of regret.

I wake up again and it's now Monday morning. Early, before school. I hear talking downstairs and go to the top of the stairs and listen. I hear my dad talking to someone in a low voice. Is he on the phone? Probably with my mom. I better call her today, or not only will she be back here but she won't leave my side for a second. The thought makes me panic slightly, but then I hear another voice. It's Julian. He must have stopped by on his way to school to check on me. I should go and say hi. Let him know I'm still alive and kicking. I run to the bathroom to spruce myself up a bit. That's when I look in the mirror and realize I can't let Julian see me like this. I'm a mess. My skin is pale gray. My eyes are red and swollen. I have splotches all over that I've never seen before. I look like I'm dying. Seeing Julian is not an option. I'll just make sure I call him first thing this afternoon.

I remember then. I run into my room and sit down at the computer. I shake it back to life and there it is. The article I was reading. I avoid looking at the picture this time and get right to the part about when they found him. I still can't believe I'm reading an article about the police finding my friend. Investigating his murder.

The autopsy suggests the body had been burned from the inside out. The article goes on to say he appeared to have suffered an extraordinary degree of burning on his torso and face, leaving his clothes singed and any facial hair gone. His mouth and eyes were burned as if the source of the heat had come from within.

It doesn't make any sense. Burned from the inside. What could cause something like that? I close the article and shut the whole computer down.

I need air.

It's still cool out but sunny. I soak in the rays and feel their effects right away. My stride quickens and I'm starting to get into a good solid pace. I run like that for a couple of miles and then head home. I am feeling better today. I guess it's like they say, you just have to take it a day at a time. I hope that's right. I hope everyday it will get easier. I hope.

Later when I get off the phone I can tell Julian was happy to hear from me. Talking to him makes me feel better. I wasn't sure how it would be, but I realize now that having him to lean on is everything. I need him.

It's the day of the funeral. The day they put my best friend in the ground.

Here come the tears again.

Part of me wants to jump back in the bed and never get out, but I can't. Julian needs me, the students and everyone expect me and Aiden may want me. Is he looking down like everyone keeps saying? Is he with us forever like I've been told? I'm not sure how I feel about any of it, but what I do know is, if any of it is true, he would want me there, so that's exactly where I'll be. There.

My parents will be at the funeral today, which gives me some comfort. Julian calls and asks if I need a ride. I don't, but I would rather ride with him, so I tell him I do. My parents really seem to be in this mellow full supportive role today. Things are starting to look somewhat bearable.

Julian drives up right on time, and I walk out as he's getting out of the car. He opens the passenger car door for me and I slide in the seat. He asks how I'm doing. All I'm able to give him is a reassuring smile. His look tells me he doesn't believe me, but he smiles back. We sit in stone silence the whole ride there. I just sit there and stare out the window. My goal today is to keep my mind blank. It's the only way I'll make it through.

We're all outside at the gravesite now. Everything until now has been a blur. So many different faces. Most I recognize from school, some I don't recognize at all. A lot of whispering and hugs. I'm numb to it all. My body is there, but my mind isn't, which I'm grateful for.

I glance around the grounds of the cemetery. Green grass, transplanted oak trees. Everything about this place reminds me of the lush surroundings of a Northern landscape. Not what you'd expect a cemetery to look like in this part of the country. Someone went to great lengths to give this place a living feel. A trick of the mind sense of comfort I suppose.

As I stand there, I feel a slight breeze blow a few strands of my hair across my face. My hands are slow to reach up and move it. Looking up I notice the leaves on the trees all around us being blown by the same breeze and try to find meaning in the movement.

Julian is standing to my left looking straight ahead. He's like a statue. Just a solid presence beside me. My parents are on my other side. My mom has her arm hooked into mine. Out of the corner of my eye, I can see her steal glances my way from time to time.

I look across the way and see Mark. Our eyes connect for just a second, but then I'm distracted by Sahara's sobbing. It's such an obnoxious spectacle. Wow, she is really outdoing herself today. She even has some friends beside her following suit. One of whom is Carissa. The image of Aiden and her walking away from me flashes in my mind.

I quickly close my eyes and focus on the wind. It's really started to pick up. The priest begins to talk then.

"I am the Resurrection. . . "

I stare at the gravesite. My numbness is breaking apart as I watch the black shiny coffin holding my best friend being lowered into the ground. The wind is really blowing now, but it doesn't keep me from feeling the tears pour down my face.

Everyone starts murmuring then: "Our father in heaven, hallowed be your name. . . "

I'm starting to shake. I can feel my heartbeat increasing. The wind is still blowing. It's whipping my hair around my head. The trees are starting to sway a bit. I stare at them and think about nothing but the way they're moving. The way the wind seems to be getting stronger. The trees are bending more. A few people gasp as the wind catches them and pushes against them. Things are starting to fly about. Tissues, leaves, and even a few hats that have gotten loose and are blowing all around. People are leaving now and leaving in a hurry. My mom yanks on my arm and I look toward her just as the first crack hits. A tree about twenty yards away is hit and then I hear the loudest rumble I've ever heard. My mom yanks again and I'm running away with her. Running away from Aiden. Running away from my life as it was before and running to a new chapter. If this storm is any indication of what's to come, I'm in trouble.

That night as I lie there playing through the images of the day in my head, I can hear my parents arguing downstairs. Until around the time my episodes started they barely even looked at each other in a cross way, but now. . .

Another strange life change to throw on the pile.

Reaching over in the dark I feel around for my phone and earphones. Maybe if I listen to some music it'll distract me from not only the faint arguing downstairs but everything that's happened lately. I just need a reprieve from my life, even if its just a quick one.

Searching through my library of music I find the one

song that always seems to lift my spirits. As its upbeat tune blasts in my ears, I close my eyes, concentrating on its rhythmic beat and melodramatic lyrics. My mind's gone, floating in that world of fantasy. That world I sometimes visit when my own seems dull. The world I haven't needed to go to in a while.

It's just a graze. A light touch across my lips.

Startled, my eyes fly open as a gasp escapes me. I quickly sit up and grab the earphones off my head in one fluid motion. My eyes scan the room, searching. The faint light of the moon enables me to see everywhere but the dark corner by my closet. I'm frozen in place as my eyes are locked on the possible hiding place, waiting for even the slightest movement. My window's slightly ajar, but it was like that before. Right? I was hot earlier and opened it. I think so.

I feel my body begin to respond to my fear. Respond appropriately? Not likely.

Could I have been imagining it? Was my mind playing tricks on me? Hell no, I know what I felt. My body may be doing some crazy things lately, but I'm not crazy. I felt someone touch my lips. Continuing to look around, I slowly lean over to turn on my lamp. I twist the knob and the entire room is illuminated. It takes my eyes two seconds to adjust, but I can see there's no one.

Even so, it takes only another minute to realize my body is at the point of no return, pushing me to respond. I'm panting now as I stare at the window. I can feel myself escalating, as all my instincts are screaming at me to move, to react. I feel like I'll combust if I don't.

I should be feeling scared, terrified even, but instead all I can think about is running, anything to get my body in motion. A strange response for a girl that thinks someone was in her room, but then, I'm not like other girls.

Devoid of any logic at this point, I throw caution to the

wind and leap out the window. Oh shit, I'm barefooted, I realize when my feet hit the ground. Too late. With my body's relentless insistence, I'm off.

It isn't until I'm back, almost an hour later, that the full ramifications of this night's events hit home. All I can do is lie in my bed and shake uncontrollably until sometime later I finally drift off to a much welcomed, restless sleep.

4

—

Mrs. Johnson, standing at the board and using a pencil to point at some numbers that are written across it, is saying something about obtuse triangles.

"In this problem, if the angle of this triangle is greater than 90 degrees and less than 180 degrees, then the other two angles would. . . "

I look up at the clock above the door. My eyes linger over its various flaws. The crack on the right side of the plastic covering. The way the number three is turned, causing it to be slightly off center. The second hand that never moves, forever stuck in between nine and ten. Sometimes as I stare at it, I find myself willing it to move, to continue on its never-ending course. Time is moving excruciatingly slowly today. I feel like I'm in prison, shackled to my seat, watching the minutes go by but feeling like they're hours. It takes everything in me to feign interest.

The last few weeks have been exhausting. Images, crazy images, will pop into my head throughout the day, causing my body to instantly react. The thought that someone might have been in my room that night still creeps me out, but I find doubt and even denial help me cope. It's the void left from losing Aiden that's always there. Grieving doesn't seem to be an option for me, though, so I wearily go through the motions of my everyday routines, mindful to keep my thoughts focused.

The bell rings, and in an instant kids are filing out of the room. I give the clock one last appreciative look and join the crowd. Walking to my locker, I feel like I'm in a fog. My symptoms are getting worse. In the three weeks since the funeral I've had a nightly episode five times and have even had a couple of small ones at school.

The last one happened at lunch. Julian and a couple of people were talking about something that had happened to a girl the day before. I was hearing bits and pieces of the story but having a really hard time keeping focused on what they were saying. My thoughts kept jumping to the murders. The police were baffled, things just didn't add up, didn't make logical sense. So they were pursuing a few different theories, at least that's what everyone was being led to believe.

As I sat there going over it all my head, I could feel my body reacting. I instantly knew I had to move, get out of there . . . change my train of thought. Anything to distract my body and keep a full-blown episode from happening. I made a quick excuse and went outside. Just walking around and being outside calmed me.

In the first few days after the funeral I had to go talk to the school counselor. She reassured me that any thoughts I may be having were completely normal. That grieving is a process and that I'm not alone. That was funny to hear, because since I had been back to school all anyone seemed to be doing was leaving me alone. I would catch people looking at me in class or around the school as if they were waiting for me to spontaneously combust or something. I had never felt so isolated and alone in all my life.

As far as my thoughts being normal, I doubt she would think that if she actually knew what I was thinking. I think back to Aiden, his behavior . . . how agitated he seemed

and what about when I touched him? He was so hot, hot like I am sometimes. It's strange.

I'm headed out to track practice. I've gotten to where I look forward to practice every day. The first few were hard without Aiden. I did have Julian there, smiling and trying hard to keep things normal, but it still took some getting used to. Now I enjoy my time outside, running, not thinking about anything in particular, just concentrating on my breathing. Feeling my heartbeat . . . smooth and steady. I have even become a better runner. I am faster and have more endurance. Even the girls on the team seem to be noticing. It's the only time of the day when I feel I'm connecting with others.

I see Coach Miller up ahead. He has his stopwatch today, which means he's checking times for the upcoming meet. Figuring out who's going to run which race based on their speed. I usually dread this drill, but today I'm feeling good about it. Knowing my times have improved, I hope to get assigned to run a leg in the relay race.

As I come up to the finish, I'm not nearly as out of breath as I usually am. I cross his invisible line, and he pushes the watch. I stop and look back. I didn't realize it, but I'm way out ahead of all the other girls. Even I'm a little puzzled by this, and by the look on his face, he is, too. "Uh . . . great job Jo," he says, giving his watch a little shake. Again he gives me a puzzled look and then walks off still shaking the watch slightly saying, "This darn thing finally broke."

The other runners are coming in now, and everyone seems to be giving me a similarly puzzled look. So much for feeling connected. I don't care. All I know is I'm feeling good today. I smile at some of the girls and turn to head back to the locker room.

Afterward I head to the parking lot. If I beat Julian out here today, I'll just sit on the hood of his precious car and get some homework done. He just loves it when I do that. When I think about the look on his face when he sees me, it makes me smile.

I look across the parking lot, but can see he's already standing there. I guess I didn't run as fast as I thought. Someone's with him. I see blond hair and a cheerleading outfit, but it can't be. What could he possibly have to say to Sahara? I slow my pace realizing that they are in some sort of argument. Sahara says something, and before I know it Julian has her pinned against the car. Her reaction is fast. I mean really fast. She throws him off, and he goes flying back with such force it sends him sailing. I start to run toward him as he stands up. He seems to be about to head back over to her but sees me and pauses. He glances in Sahara's direction as I run up to him. "Are you all right?" I say as I look him up and down searching for the injury that I know he must have gotten from that kind of fall.

"I'm fine," he says, brushing off my attempts to give him a check-over. I look over toward Sahara, but she's gone. "What the hell was that?" I shout, starting to shake slightly. He turns around and gives me one of those Julian smiles and says, "Jo, it really was nothing. Just a misunderstanding."

"A misunderstanding?" I yell at him. "A misunderstanding is 'oops, I didn't realize you wanted the last piece of pie.' Not throwing someone through the air. How the hell did she do that?" I'm looking at him now in disbelief. What did I just witness? Julian is much bigger and heavier than her, yet she'd thrown him as if he were some small kid or something.

He gets in the car, but I just stand by the passenger-side door for a minute. When I get in, he takes off, cranking the radio louder than usual. I reach over and shut it off. I'm pissed. Why is Julian acting like it wasn't a big deal?

"So you aren't going to tell me what that was all about?" I say angrily.

"Jo, it really wasn't as big of a deal as it may have looked. You know me—my mouth can sometimes get me in trouble."

"What could you have possibly said to cause that?" I say, not believing a word he's telling me.

"I honestly don't know, I mean, I say things all the time. I guess whatever it was really rubbed her the wrong way. You know Sahara—she's like a walking soap opera."

I just sit there looking at him. Does he think I believe this load of crap? He obviously doesn't want me to know what's really going on, but why? What could Sahara know about Julian that I don't? I really don't need to be dealing with this right now. I don't care about Sahara, but how exactly she was able to throw him the way she did? Whatever. I just want to be alone and I especially want to be away from Julian.

I stare out the passenger window the rest of the ride home. When we pull up to my house I move to get out of the car without a word, but Julian grabs my arm.

"Please Jo, trust me. It wasn't a big deal. There's nothing going on here that I'm not telling you. Sahara was pissed, and when she started in on me I guess things just got out of hand."

"But how was she able to throw you?" I ask.

"I honestly don't know, but I'm totally fine," he says with an expression I find uncomfortable. "I can't have you mad at me. With everything that's happened, you and I really only have each other. You're my best friend, Jo, and I won't let anything change that."

He's looking at me now with such heartfelt sincerity that my resolve just breaks down. I need him now more than ever. Although in the back of my head I'm not sure if I truly believe him, I know that I want to. I need to.

I smile slightly, reassuring him that our friendship is still intact. "Well, as long as you're not hurt, I. . . "

"I'm not, I promise. No Buffy the Vampire cheerleader is going to get the best of me," he says and laughs.

That night I lie there unable to sleep as my mind is riddled with crazy thoughts. Thinking back to the night I had my first episode, I go over all the things that have happened over the last couple of months in my head. My mind drifts to Julian. I think about our friendship. I've never been as close to him as I was to Aiden. I just haven't known him as long, so, I guess how could I be? After what happened today, though, I just can't shake the feeling that there's way more to him than I know.

I sit up in bed. I need a break. Need to clear my head. As usual I'm dressed in shorts and a tank top in case I find myself going for a middle-of-the-night run.

At least I'm always prepared.

I open my window and peer out. It's quiet and dark. I try to look down the street from here to see Mark's house, but the curve in the street is too sharp. I climb out the window and use the large branch to get in the tree. My room's on the second floor, but I conveniently have a large eucalyptus tree right outside my window. One of the only types of large trees that are naturally found in this part of the country. I love this tree. I've climbed it so many times I don't even give it a second thought. I sit in the tree for a few minutes just taking in the sounds of the night. So peaceful.

Quickly I move down the tree and hop to the ground. It's strange being out here but not having an episode. I get an uneasy feeling. Part of me wants to go back up the tree into my room, but the thought of being up there alone with my thoughts stops me.

Walking down the street, I'm jolted out of my thoughts by a noise behind me. I look back but see nothing but darkness, shadows, and the occasional porch light. The hair on the back of my neck stands up, and I instantly regret not listening to that part of myself that said to go back in when I had the chance.

I keep walking toward Mark's house, hoping he's outside. I'm not really thinking about how I'm going to explain being out here, but right now, I really don't care.

At this point I know I'm definitely not alone. Again I hear a noise come from back behind me by a house to my left. The house is dark. With a wood fence, cars in the driveway, and the house itself, I realize there are lots of places for someone to hide. I pick up my pace. I think that maybe I should just turn around and run back home, but I'd have to run right in front of the house—where the noise came from. Not an option.

I can see Mark's house now, and the light is on. I take off toward it.

I see him now.

 See him with the ball, then making a shot.

I run up to him just as he's turning around toward me. He's startled. I turn around and half expect to see someone running down the street after me, but there's no one. Just darkness. There's nothing.

I turn back around, and Mark is looking down the street, too. I can tell he understands. "Are you ok?" he says.

I'm out of breath but I manage to say, "I am now."

Taking my arm, he leads me toward his house. We go inside and stand in his kitchen. "What happened?" he asks as he pulls a chair out for me to sit in. I'm shaking. Going to the fridge, he gets a bottle of water out and places it in front of me. I watch as he pulls a chair out and sits down very close facing me. He seems genuinely concerned as he leans forward and takes my hands in his. Normally just having him hold my hands would have sent me into orbit, but right now I barely notice it.

I gaze into those beautiful brown eyes of his. I've been lucky tonight, in more ways than one.

He grabs the water and holds it out for me. "Here, try to drink something," he says, probably trying to get me to stop staring at him and react in some way. That seems to break the spell, and I take the water and drink some. The cold liquid revives me a bit.

"Feeling better?" he says without taking his eyes off of me.

"Yes, thanks," I say, giving him a weak smile.

"What happened out there?"

"Um, well . . . I was having some trouble sleeping, so I thought I'd just take a quick walk, clear my head a little."

I realize as I say it how foolish it sounds. Why would a girl my age decide just to go for a walk in the middle of the night? Especially with everything that's been going on. I wait for him to say something about that or give me a crazy look, but he doesn't. He doesn't seem to judge at all.

"Once I got down the street, I heard a noise and thought someone was following me. I guess it freaked me out, so when I saw your light on I ran over here."

Looking at him now I have an overwhelming fear that he probably thinks I'm stupid. . . or just plain nuts. I suddenly feel the need to explain myself. Before I know it, I'm telling him everything. Everything about the episodes I'm having. About the night running. About how I suspected Aiden might have been suffering from the same symptoms. How nothing about the murders seems to add up. I don't tell him about the nights I've sat watching him play. I figure I'm registering high on his crazy-person scale right now, so I'll leave out my stalking stories.

When I'm finished with my verbal explosion, I just stop and stare into those eyes. I'm waiting for him to stand up and laugh, call the cops. . . who knows. Instead he takes my hands again and without even a flinch says, "I'm sorry all this is happening to you and I'm sorry you've had to go through these things alone, but not anymore. I'm here for you Jo. No matter what, I'll help you through this."

I want to cry then. I want to throw my arms around him and never let go.

Waking up, I feel more rested than I have in a while. Last night after Mark brought me back and reassured me, I slept, and slept soundly. I play back our conversation in my head. Now I don't have to feel so isolated. I have someone I can talk to, and it feels great.

With this new sense of solace, I decide I'm going to do something I've been wanting to do but just . . . couldn't. I'm going to go see Aiden.

When I get to the cemetery, I am instantly taken back to that day. It's been almost a month since the day of the storm. Everything looks different now. The trees are still . . . peaceful. As I look around, I can't help but think if there was anywhere I had to pick as my final resting place, this would be it. It's perfect.

I walk over to the back of the property by the tree line. I really have no idea how I'm able to remember where to go, but before I know it, I'm standing in front of a gravestone with my friend's name on it. It's hard to imagine that he's actually here. Here in this very spot, deep beneath the ground, in that obnoxiously shiny coffin.

"I miss you, Aiden. I've been so lonely without you." The tears start coming then, and I start to feel that same hollow feeling in my gut. I concentrate on the feeling, hoping to calm myself down a bit. Taking a deep breath, I continue.

"I'm sorry. So sorry this happened to you. I never . . . never imagined my future without you in it. I just want . . . just need you to know . . ."

My mind goes blank as I feel a flood of emotions rise to the surface, threatening to send me back to that dark place, that same place I had just recently managed to crawl out of. I look up at the trees. I'm seeking their comfort once again. This time, though, they give me nothing.

I have so many things I want to say. So much I need to say but I can't.

I feel a hand on my shoulder and turn around quickly. He's here. He's here for me just like he said he would be. Next thing I know I'm in his arms. He's impossibly tall. He strokes my head as I cry. After a while I know it's time to say good-bye.

I couldn't be in better hands.

5

—

The bell rings and I jump. Everybody is starting to file out of the room, so I stand up and gather my books. I must have dozed off a little. It's strange that I'm so tired. These past couple of weeks since that day at the gravesite I've been sleeping better than I have in a while. The night episodes have all but stopped, and the little ones I have throughout the day have become manageable. Things seem to be turning around.

Julian and I are pretty much back to normal. I realize now how little time we ever really spent together just the two of us. Our rides back and forth to school are almost the only times we have together alone. I enjoy those rides. He's fun and easy to be around. Neither one of us has brought up that afternoon. Although it still bugs me when I think about it, it's easier to move on. He seems glad I have and is back to being his annoyingly cocky self.

As I walk to my locker, I notice all the familiar faces passing me by. I guess the novelty of Aiden's death has worn off. Everyone is back to treating me as they did before. There's an occasional uninterested smile, but mostly they ignore me. It's still better than being treated like you're an emotional time bomb.

I'm standing at my locker trying to remember what books I need to take home when Mark appears. "Hey, how's everything going?"

My heart skips a beat as I look up into the eyes that I have luckily grown accustomed to seeing. Ever since that night when I spilled my guts, he has been nothing but true to his word. He usually swings by my locker a couple of times a day. I also catch him looking my way a lot more often in the lunchroom. I guess I gave him one more thing in his life that he needs to take care of . . . to look after. Part of me feels guilty, but I want him in my life. I want this thing that has started between us to continue.

Giving him a big smile, I say, "Everything's good."

"That's great," he says and looks knowingly at me. We just stand there like that for a few seconds, both wanting to say more but not being able to. With prying ears around and all. Looking down at his feet, he seems uncomfortable.

"Any plans this weekend?" he asks.

I can tell there's something on his mind, but how do I ask? I want to ask, but it's these kind of awkward moments that I've never been good with.

"I'm looking forward to spending the weekend with Nick, Jay, and Daisy." He gives me a surprised look.

"Hanging out with some friends?"

"Yeah, if you call writing my term paper on The Great Gatsby hanging out," I say with a big grin.

He laughs then and says, "Well, I hope you guys have a good time."

He lingers for a moment before saying good-bye. I just stand there and look into my locker. All I can think is . . . what a huge wuss I am.

How the heck am I supposed to write this stupid paper if the only thing I can think about is Mark. I've been sitting here staring at my computer for two hours. I keep thinking about the way he acted at my locker yesterday. He really seemed to have something on his mind. Why didn't I just ask?

Irritated, I push away from the computer and decide I need a break. I go downstairs and find my parents in the office talking quietly. They normally love to discuss work-related issues and bounce ideas off each other. It's great that they have a relationship where they can do that, and I would actually find their back and forth cute if it weren't so darn boring. Today's different. Their tone, demeanor even, suggests an edge to the conversation. It has to be the stress of the recent murders. Even though they haven't been particularly more protective of me lately, I know something's bothering them.

I peek around the door and say, "I'm going for a walk." Seemingly surprised, they both turn around.

"How's the paper coming?" my dad asks with a weak smile.

"It's coming. I just need a break," I say and head toward the door.

My mom yells out, "Remember, your dad and I are leaving soon for the fund-raiser, so I put your dinner in the fridge."

"Oh right . . . thanks, and have fun!" I say as I walk out the door.

I figure they could use a little privacy right now. Besides, I have to do something if I ever want to get this paper done. A little exercise will get the creative juices flowing. I always think better when I'm moving. I start going over the book in my head as I walk in the direction of Mark's house.

As I get closer to his house, I see him and his brother, Harrison, out playing a game of one-on-one. It's cute to watch them play together. His brother is about two years younger than him, almost like a slightly smaller version.

When I stop in front of his house to watch them, Mark sees me and waves me over.

"Hey, how's that term paper coming?"

"Not so good. Thought I'd take a walk and try to jump-start my thoughts."

He passes the ball my way and asks, "How about a little game to get the blood pumping?"

I catch the ball and stand there smiling at him with no idea at all what I'm supposed to do with it. Harrison quickly swipes the ball from me, turns around, and makes a basket.

"Oh, I see how this is," I say, laughing at the boy smiling back at me. I go toward him and try to pull the same move on him. No such luck. He quickly moves around me, dribbling the ball the whole time. I try many times, to no avail, to knock the ball from his grasp but just when my hand comes near it, he's already gone, already shooting the ball toward the basket and most times making it in. I know I must look slow and clumsy running around in circles.

Next thing I know Mark's there easily taking the ball from him and putting him in his place. "All right buddy, you and Jo against me. First one to ten wins."

Harrison and I quickly develop a strategy. He does everything that involves contact with the ball, and I try to block Mark. Needless to say, it's impossible.

I can tell Mark's being easy on us. If he weren't, I would never be able to keep his huge frame from doing too much of anything. As I jump around in front of him with my arms flailing about, Harrison manages to make a basket. We go on like that for a little while, Harrison making a few baskets while I bump into Mark. He's tall and strong and just laughs as I attempt to keep him from getting to Harrison. I push against his stomach and realize how hard it is. We're so impossibly close. Just that quick contact with him awakens feelings within me. As we continue to play, his hands graze my arms, shoulders, waist. His hands seem to linger longer after every touch, even when I turn around to watch Harrison shoot the ball. His hand resting on my arm causes electricity to course through my body. His touches are gentle, almost caressing in nature. We both take advantage of the situation. I can feel myself wanting to touch him more, to graze his stomach, his arms, chest. Our goal is quickly becoming less about the game and more about physical contact. A few times our feet barely move at all, and we just spend the time pushing against each other with feigned attempts to even seem like we're playing the game. I steal a glance up at him, and he looks back at me without even a hint of a smile. All I see is longing.

If we were at a different time, a different place. . .

"You guys gonna play or what?" Harrison asks, standing there holding the ball.

We step back from each other and laugh slightly. Embarrassed, I look down at the ground while Mark runs over and in one fluid motion strips the ball from Harrison and does a perfect layup.

"Harrison, time to come in!" Mark's mom calls out from the door.

"You want to come inside for a drink?" Mark asks.

"Uh . . . sure," I say.

As we get closer to the door I'm increasingly unsure of how to act. I'm walking into his private world. A world I've heard a lot about.

Stepping into the kitchen, I realize how different it looks today than it did that night. That night. Just thinking about it gives me the chills.

"Well, hi Jo, I haven't seen you in ages."

"Oh hi, Mrs. Young, how are you?" I say giving her one of my sweet smiles. I haven't seen her up close for years. I remember her being absolutely beautiful. I can see now the years haven't been kind, but even so, she's still a beautiful woman. Tall with the same dark hair as her boys but with striking green eyes. The same eyes as Harrison.

"Can't complain really," she says and then pauses before continuing, "Jo, I just want to tell you how sorry I am about your friend. If you ever need to talk, please know my door is always open to you."

I feel a lump in my throat and my eyes start to water slightly as I look back at that gaze that's all too familiar. Although the eye color is completely different, I realize then, where Mark gets that way of looking into your very soul. All I can do is smile back at her.

She quickly changes the subject and asks, "I'm not planning anything special, but would you like to have dinner with us tonight?"

I glance over at Mark, and he's looking back at me smiling. He seems to think this is a good idea. "Well, I wouldn't want to impose. . . "

"Nonsense. We would love to have you," she says and walks away, calling out to Harrison to set another place at the table. I look at Mark.

"Your mom is really sweet."

He smiles when I say this, and I can tell it makes him happy to have someone else see this side of her. When I think of how the rumors always portray her, I realize how unfair and mean people can be.

I end up having a wonderful time at dinner, and afterward we all hang around together in the living room and watch a show. I hardly ever watch TV, so Harrison thinks it's funny that I haven't ever seen this particular show.

A month ago, I would have never believed that I'd be spending time with Mark and his family. They are really sweet with each other and seem especially close. I realize now why he's so protective.

My parents and I are close, but not in the same easygoing, hanging-out kind of way. I know they love me and would do anything for me, but they aren't as involved in my day-to-day life. My mind jumps to the assumption that it's because I'm adopted, but I quickly dismiss that as being ridiculous. My parents were very involved in their careers when they decided to adopt me. Even having a child didn't change that. Hasn't changed that.

After the show, Mark's mom gives some excuse why she needs Harrison upstairs with her. I'm slightly embarrassed but grateful at the same time. I thank her for the dinner and say goodnight.

Then I'm alone with him.

Reacting in my usual fashion to an uncomfortable situation, I quickly blurt out the first thing that comes to mind. "What's Sahara up to tonight?"

I regret saying it the moment it's out of my mouth.

He looks at me oddly but says, "Um, things haven't really been going all that well with us lately. Heck, I'm not even sure they ever did."

I want to kick myself for bringing it up.

"Oh. . . I'm sorry," I say, not meaning a word.

We just look at each other awkwardly. If I could just learn to keep my mouth shut. . .

"So how have you been feeling lately? I mean with the episode thing?" he asks.

"Since I went to Aiden's grave . . . things seemed to have settled down quite a bit," I say, my voice shaking slightly, as I think back to that day.

"When my dad left us, I remember feeling mostly sad and alone. I know I was just a kid, so I couldn't really grasp what was going on, but what I did know was that this person that I loved was here one day and gone the next. I just couldn't wrap my head around it . . . heck, I still can't. But, I moved on . . . had to. Figured I had my mom and Harrison to think about. Not only them, though. I had to think about myself . . . how I have my whole life to live. How I won't let any one incident define me. I mean, it's part of who I am for sure, but it's not . . . who I am."

I can see a little bit of what he's been through. How alone he really must have felt. He really does understand loss.

"I'm so sorry," I say.

What else can I say?

He looks at me and something switches over. His mood lightens and he says, "You know, it's strange. It really doesn't make any sense why he left. I mean all the memories I have of him are good ones. Just him as a loving father. Honestly, I think that's why my mom has never been able to let go. She truly loved him and still does. It's weird, one day he's here with us and the next he's gone. No note, nothing. Just monthly deposits into our bank account. Non-traceable, and believe me, I've tried. It's as if he still wants to take care of us . . . just not be with us."

I think of my dad then and how lucky I am. I'm not even his biological child, yet he's there for me. I mean, he may not always actually be there, but I've never felt abandoned, only loved and wanted. I can hear my mom's words in my head now, "We may not have given birth to you, but . . . we wanted you." I understand these words now more than ever.

The clock chimes on the wall, and I jump at the sound. It's getting late, and I remember the term paper waiting for me at home. As if he's reading my thoughts, he stands up and says, "I guess I better walk you home. Your parents will think I kidnapped you."

"They're at some work thing tonight for my dad. The university is trying to raise more money for something," I say and smile.

"That's the school I want to get a basketball scholarship to. That way, I could go to college but still be close to home for my brother." His voice sounds so determined. At that moment I have no doubt that Mark will accomplish everything that he sets his mind to.

As we walk to my house he tells me all about how he's gotten roped into participating with the rest of the basketball team in the end-of-year talent show. Although he seems anything but thrilled, it does sound like it's going to be a pretty funny skit.

When we get to my house, I see my parents are still out. The sun's gone down since I've left, so it's dark inside. I walk up to the door and take the key out of the very secret hiding place under the planter to the right. Mark laughs at this and says something about our crack security system. Normally I would have some sort of comeback about how safe our neighborhood is, but instead I'm left feeling somewhat uneasy.

Mark picks up on this and insists he come in to look around before leaving me. Mark in my house . . . with nobody home. Nothing has ever sounded so good.

I walk in first with him following close behind. I flip every light switch I come across. After being in his cozy house with its carpet, curtains, and kid things all around, my house seems like a small, frigid museum. Hardwood floors end to end with oriental rugs placed perfectly proportionate with the furniture. Plantation shutters on every window covered with ornate window dressings. Pieces of actual, never-to-be-touched artwork dispersed evenly throughout.

My parents have always been neat freaks. They never childproofed the house. I always just assumed it was because they didn't get me until they were set in their ways.

As we go from room to room checking everything, I realize how cold and uninviting my house really is. I guess it explains why I practically live in my room. It's the one place I feel the most at home within my entire house.

I think of my room now and how I've always thought of it as my own private oasis. As we go upstairs, my heart begins to race slightly. I'm going to have Mark in my room. I mean, Aiden and Julian have been in there tons of times, usually making fun of my things, but this is different. This is Mark. The person I've dreamt of having in my room a million times . . . of doing things with in my room a million times.

My heart is definitely racing and I'm beginning to feel hot. I'm starting to feel that terrible familiar feeling.

Oh no, not now. . .

We walk into my room, and he starts to look around. I stand back by the door just trying to concentrate on breathing. Why is this happening now? Of all times. He turns around then.

"Everything looks . . . Jo, what's wrong?" he asks, coming toward me. He takes my arm but quickly draws his hand away. "You're burning up!" he says. By this time I can feel my heart racing and I'm getting antsy. Really antsy. "I'm going to get you a cold washcloth," he says and starts to leave the room. I react fast. Faster than I ever have.

I grab his arm and throw him on the bed as if he weighs no more than a small child. I feel strength course through my body, and at that moment there's only one thing I want . . . him. I'm on top of him. Straddling him before I know what's happening. I bend down to kiss him. Kiss him with all the passion and longing I've felt for him for so long. To devour him. To take him as my own.

I freeze. I see him then. His eyes are confused but his body is holding onto me with the same wanting. We stay like this, looking into each other's eyes. Not understanding really how we ended up here.

I jump up and run to the bathroom. I slam the door behind me as I run to the sink. I splash cold water on my face, hoping it will bring me out of this crazy episode.

I try to concentrate on my breathing. To focus my thoughts on a towel that's hanging there. Blue and white threads interwoven in a specific pattern. I reach out and grab the towel, rubbing it against my face. I'm feeling calmer now. More in control. When I look in the mirror, I hardly recognize the person starting back at me. My skin is flawless, almost glowing. The imperfections that I normally see are gone. I stand there in amazement, my eyes shining back at me with a similar glow. Their bluish-green color vivid and sparkling like tiny replicas of the Mediterranean Sea. I blink but everything stays the same. I stare at my reflection unable to comprehend not only what I see, but what just happened in my room. Will he still be there, or was he smart and took off the first chance he got?

I head back to my room.

There's Mark, sitting on the edge of my bed just staring out. When he sees me, he stands up and walks toward me. The next thing I know he has his arms around me, hugging me tight.

I hug him back and whisper, "I'm so sorry."

He laughs then and looks at me. "You have nothing to be sorry about. Really I'm kinda sorry you ran out," he says with a twinkle in his eye.

I'm floored by this. He can actually find humor in my display of craziness.

There's hope for us yet.

6

The horn honks and I'm running out the door. As I get in the car, I give Julian a big grin.

"Hey."

"Well, aren't you in an especially good mood for a Monday," Julian says, eyeing me as if I were up to something.

I want to tell him everything. Everything about the evening I spent with Mark and his family, about my crazier than normal episode—everything. But I can't. Ever since that afternoon with Sahara, I haven't completely trusted him.

"I finished my stinking term paper."

"Oh yeah, how is Mr. Gatsby anyway?" he says with a slight laugh.

"So what did you do this weekend? Cause a ruckus at the country club by showing up with a stripper?"

"Ha, ha. I wish. No, I had to perform at some charity event for my mom, and you know how much I hate those things."

Julian hates to perform. He would much rather just be at home composing or playing one of his new compositions for Aiden and I. Come to think of it, I haven't heard him play since Aiden's death. He probably knows I'd have a hard time sitting in that room, on that couch, without Aiden there. Or maybe he's the one who would have a harder time.

"This is the good part," he says and reaches over and cranks up the radio. I laugh as he begins to obnoxiously sing the words.

No, maybe Aiden's death didn't bother him as much as I thought it would, or maybe Julian is just being typical

Julian.

English Lit class is a breeze this week. Mr. Geary is having everyone present their term papers.

A girl named Samantha just finished her presentation on the book Great Expectations, and I can honestly say I didn't hear a word she said. I mindlessly clap as she takes her seat. Now Mr. Geary is standing at the front of the class calling up one of the boys who sits in the back. He's one of a group of three punk kids that hang around together, all looking older than your average eleventh grader. I'll sometimes see them out in the parking lot after track practice or over by the bleachers. They always have that up-to-no-good look, but I really don't pay much attention to them.

Now the one named Declan is being summoned by the teacher to come up and give his presentation. This should be good.

"Declan, if you're unable to give your presentation today, then I'm going to have to take ten points off your final grade," Mr. Geary says in that stern teacher voice.

"I wrote that paper, but I ain't standing up there saying nothing," Declan says with disdain in his voice.

"I'd watch your tone, young man," Mr. Geary says, now having moved closer to Declan's seat. Just then one of the boys sitting in the front of the class snickers. It's Nick, one of the football players. I don't know much about the game, but by the looks of him he's probably one of those guys that do the blocking. He's really the only person in class I would even expect to mess with these guys.

"You got something to say, dickhead?" Declan says as

he stands up and moves toward Nick's seat. Nick abruptly stands up and turns to face him.

Mr. Geary, probably sensing things about to get out of control, puts himself between the two boys.

"Yeah asshole, why don't you get up there and do your presentation like everyone else. Or do you need some sort of special Ed excuse or something?" Nick says.

I look over as Declan's two buddies stand up.

"Guys, settle down, and you two—back in your seats!" Mr. Geary says, pointing to the two friends in back.

Nobody makes a move as Declan and Nick just stand there glaring at each other.

"Fun's over. Now get back in your seats! All of you!" Mr. Geary yells.

You can tell Declan's not one to react well when being yelled at. "Or what, old man?" Declan says making a move toward him.

My heart's racing. I realize I'm on my way to having a full-blown episode. If I can control my breathing, maybe no one will even notice. I turn around and face the front of the classroom to take my mind off of what's happening. As I'm sitting there concentrating on my breathing, something changes.

It's the movement that catches my attention.

Nick takes a step toward Mr. Geary. Maybe he wants to put himself between them, or maybe he's just making his way straight for Declan. Who knows? But what I do know is, Declan sees him coming and makes a move to hit Mr. Geary.

I'm there. I'm there before anyone including myself realizes it. I block the punch aimed at Mr. Geary and send Declan reeling back. I'm instantly on the two friends, who are already headed my way. The first one I hit with such a force that blood splatters across his friend, who I promptly send sailing. I'm fast. Faster than seems possible. I fight as if

I had been training for years.

My senses heightened, I can feel myself radiating heat. My heartbeat and breathing has actually slowed to an extremely slow steady rhythm. I just stand here feeling that steady heartbeat . . . barely breathing. How am I not out of breath?

"Josephine," Mr. Geary says and puts his hand on my shoulder.

I run then. I run out of the room. I run down the hall and into the girls' bathroom. As I burst through the door, I startle two girls that are in there. I barely look at them and run into a stall and slam the door shut.

"Freak," I hear one of the girls say before exiting the bathroom.

I put my face in my hands. Yes, I am a freak. There's no doubt about that.

I sit in a stall through two bell rings. I know I'm supposed to be in my next class, but I can't leave. I'm certain by now it's all over the school. Jo, the freak.

How am I ever going to explain this?

I hear the bathroom door open and then a familiar voice asks, "Going to stay in there all day?" It's Julian. Of everyone, I'm not surprised he would be the one to find me. I hear him go into the stall next to me and start peeing.

"Julian! I mean . . . really?" I say to him as I leave the stall. He's coming out zipping himself up.

"Well, I had to get you out of there," he says.

I laugh then and give him a slight push.

He steps back and with a big grin says, "Settle down now, I heard you have a mean right hook."

"Ugh, I don't know what happened. I don't know how I . . . I guess I just thought Mr. Geary might get hurt or something. . . "

"So you thought you'd step in and protect him? Between those thugs and the wooly mammoth? Really, that's what you were thinking?" he asks in disbelief.

It's as if he's sizing me up or something. "How did you do that, Jo?"

"I honestly don't know. I guess the adrenalin got me going," I say, knowing very well the look I'm about to get from him.

And, there it is . . . that look.

"Well, ninja master, I believe we are both late for our next class, and you will probably be getting a special VIP invitation to the principal's office. By the way, when you go, tell Mr. Quinn I said hello, would you?" And with that Julian gives me a huge grin and escorts me out of the bathroom.

Mr. Quinn sits there eyeing me. Being that this is the first time I've ever been to the principal's office, I'm surprised at how calm I am.

He's a short, overweight man. He has red hair combed over in such a way that no matter how you look at him, your eyes automatically go to his head. I'm amazed at how perfectly uniform every strand of hair is, lying in an exact line running horizontal along his brow line.

He speaks first. "So, care to elaborate on the events that lead up to that disruption in class?"

I sink down a little in my seat. "No. . . I mean, I was just trying to help Mr. Geary," I say and shrug.

He squints his eyes at me.

"You were just helping Mr. Geary, huh? Well, I'd like to know how all those boys got hurt?"

"I must have learned more from my self-defense class than I thought," I say, getting more annoyed by the minute.

"Self-defense class?" he asks, then sighs.

Not sure what's going to happen to me and not really caring much, I just sit there studying the amazing feat of physics that's his hair.

When I walk out of the office, Julian is there to greet me. We walk down the hall headed to the locker rooms to change for track practice.

"So are you going to be joining the janitorial staff on their daily litter pick up?" he asks.

I smile at him and say, "Actually, I've been let off for good behavior. I guess since I have no priors he's letting this pass."

He looks at me incredulity, "Really . . . Mr. Quinn never lets anyone just go free! What did you do, give him hair tips or something?" he says and laughs.

That afternoon when I get home, I finally get a chance to run through everything that happened in my head. It was if my body had been on autopilot. I'd reacted before I even realized what I was doing. Maybe I'm possessed.

I hear my cell phone start singing its familiar tune and

realize I left it downstairs. The house phone rings then and I hear my dad call up that it's for me. I really hope it's not Julian calling to mess with me again. Does he ever quit?

My dad's holding the phone and mouthing to me that it's Mark. Just the person I need to talk to right now. I take the phone from him and then give him that look that says get lost. He laughs and goes back into his office.

After I hang up with Mark, I do feel better. I guess the story had changed somewhat from what really happened. It didn't make me seem too freakish. Just more badass. Not that I like the attention, but if I had to be labeled one or the other, I'll take it.

I look over at Julian and laugh as he sings. It's Saturday night and we're on our way to the fair. When he called this morning to see if I wanted to go I almost passed, but now I'm glad I did. It's the first time in a while I've felt like going out and doing something.

The stereo is blasting, and every once in a while he rocks out on his air drums. He looks over and gives me a big grin. He's in a great mood, and as I sit there, I notice how handsome he looks. He's in a dark blue button-down that has one button open lower than usual. His hair has gotten longer and wavier and is rumpled and loose around his head. His blue eyes seem to flash. Julian and I have had our ups and downs lately, but when he's in one of these playful moods I find it hard not to enjoy being around him.

He turns the volume down and touches my hand. "I'm glad you came tonight, Jo."

I feel the warmth of his hand.

"You know, I am, too," I say smiling at him. "I haven't been to the fair since I was a little kid."

"Well, missy, you are in for a treat," he says with a mischievous look in his eyes. "They have got some crazy rides now."

"Oh no, don't you even think about it. You know I hate those things."

He just laughs, but I can tell he's concocting a plan even as I sit here. Oh boy, going to the fair with Julian . . . what was I thinking?

We pull into the fairground and it's packed with cars. The sun has already set, so it's dark out. We're guided into our parking space by a man with a glowing baton. I had forgotten how crowded these places can get. Julian pulls in the space and turns the car off.

"You ready to have a little fun?" he asks smiling at me.

"I am, as long as you remember who you're with." Revolving buckets extend toward the sky in the distance. I watch them go around and around all the while flashing an array of obnoxious lights. I point at the ride. "I'm the person you will never get to go on that."

"Oh Jo, I would never expect you to go on that one," he says with a wink.

The rides have gotten crazier since the last time I was here. Night of fun, here I come.

As we walk through the entrance, the music is pounding. There are flashing lights and people everywhere. It's like an experiment on sensory overload. Julian heads straight up to the ticket booth and buys two wristbands. I offer him my money, but as usual he refuses. I hate it when he pays for stuff. I know his family has tons of money but it always makes me feel weird.

He fastens the wristband on me then rubs his hands together and says, "Let the games begin," laughing his most evil laugh.

I just roll my eyes and follow him as we make our way to some sort of spinning contraption. It looks like one of those spaceships from the old movies, except for the extremely loud rock music coming from it. As I watch the people in front of me get on, I realize this is my chance to bail. I look over at Julian, but just before the words can escape my mouth he's grabbed my hand and we're boarding.

I swallow my apprehension and sit down next to him on some sort of metal seat. He looks over and grins as he says something, but the music is so loud all I get is something about G's.

A bar comes down and locks us into place. I'm going to kill Julian when this is over. . .

After the spaceship from hell, we head over to the balloon dart game. After that last ride I think Julian figured he better not push his luck.

We get to the game just as a couple of girls about my age are shelling out their money to the questionable person running it. He yanks the bills out of their hands and stuffs them into his pockets as his eyes rove over the more abundant chest of the two girls. He hands them their darts and they proceed to miss all the balloons but one. The attendant seems happy with the outcome, and seeing me eye a stuffed tiger that's hanging, he quickly looks to me to become his next victim.

Julian steps forward, and right away I see the reaction the two girls have when they see him. Inside I'm rolling my eyes as I watch them giggle and bat their eyelashes like a couple of idiots. I know that he's a great-looking guy and goes out with a lot of girls, it's just I never think of him like that. Whenever girls have this reaction to him, it always takes me off guard or, in this case, makes me want to vomit. He buys the darts from the attendant and hands them to me.

"Oh no, you're going to win me that stuffed tiger as punishment for taking me on the space ride from hell," I say raising my eyebrows and giving him that don't mess with me look.

He laughs. "Ok, ok. But I have to say, seeing your face was worth it."

Then, to the delight of the girls still standing there watching him, he throws his darts and with perfect accuracy hits all targets. The stuffed tiger is mine.

"Now that's the way you do it," I hear a voice purr from behind us. I turn around but already know who it is. Sahara and that girl Carissa from the party are standing behind us. Seeing Carissa sends a strange electric sensation through me.

"You guys here on a date or what?" Sahara asks, never taking her eyes off Julian.

What is this thing between the two of them? I can feel the tension in the air when they're around each other, and Julian instantly starts acting unusual.

Mark walks up, and all my anger toward Carissa is swept away as I look up at him. His brown eyes seem to light up momentarily when he sees me. He's wearing a black shirt that is just tight enough to show off his well-defined chest and arms. He's taller than everyone around us, which gives him a more commanding presence.

"Hi Mark," I say in a pleasantly surprised tone, ignoring the two he's with.

"Hey guys," he says looking at me oddly.

Sahara starts blabbing on and on about what they've been doing since they've been here, who they have been running into from school. All the while she's talking, Julian is quiet and I can see Mark glancing at me from time to time.

Then, I think more to get her to shut up than anything, Mark interrupts her to suggest we all go in the funhouse or go do something . . . anything. I agree right away. Julian shoots me a look but reluctantly agrees, and we're all off in the direction of the funhouse.

The fair is huge. Every year it's set up in the same gigantic open field, isolated from the rest of the city or surrounding areas. Basically, a piece of underdeveloped desert, where the closest thing to it is the airport.

It's one of the big attractions of the year, which means almost everybody at my school makes at least one trip out here over the course of the five days it's in town. As we walk through the crowd, I recognize a few different groups of students scattered around. As we come up on one such group, Sahara lets out what sounds something like a squeal of delight and bounds off, with Carissa right behind her. Mark and I ploddingly follow them while Julian decides this is a great time to grab some food.

"I'm glad I ran into you," Mark says sweetly.

I have to ask.

"So, you and Sahara have worked things out?"

"No. I had actually gone over to her house tonight to talk about things, and somehow ended up here. Let's just say, she's not the best listener," he says looking in her direction.

Her mouth is going a mile a minute. Even though a small part of me is amazed, I'm mostly irritated at the amount of energy Sahara is willing to expend on gossip. I've never been one to care much about what people are doing. I have a hard enough time dealing with my own life. As I stand there listening to her blather on, Julian walks up with a big plate of what looks like fried crust.

My stomach roils as he shoves the plate under my nose.

"Want a bite?" he says with his mouth full.

"Ugh. . . how can you eat that?"

"What? You can't come here and not partake in the local delicacies."

I just give him a disgusted look, and then as if on cue Mark suggests we head on to the funhouse. It seems following Sahara around is getting on his nerves as much as it is mine. When he tells her we're headed over, she barely stops talking and just shrugs at him.

The funhouse is on the far left corner of the fair, almost off by itself, which adds to the whole creepiness factor. At that moment all I can think about is those stupid slasher movies where someone, usually a dumb teenage girl, gets stabbed to death as she makes her way through a maze of disturbingly gross rooms. Why am I going in here again?

"You know, why don't you two go ahead, and I'll wait by the exit," I say, trying to sound nonchalant so Julian doesn't pick up on the fact that I'm feeling totally creeped out.

"Nice try, Jo," he says and then starts to look around slowly.

Mark chimes in, "You know . . . there's not many people around out here, so . . . uh, you're probably safer with us inside," he says, trying not to smile.

I glance around. He's right.

I look up at the funhouse. Once you get past the flashing lights and scary clown theme, you can see that the actual structure itself is worn and decrepit. I wonder how many people have walked through it. Have been just as creeped out as I am right now but went ahead and climbed those rickety stairs in anticipation of a chilling thrill.

Against my better judgment but not wanting to come across as a total wuss, I walk up and show my wristband to the strange-looking man who seems to be in charge of this place. I can only assume that the people responsible for operating this fair decided to hire the most demented person I've ever seen to add to the creepiness of this attraction. After half glancing at my wrist, he turns to look at Mark's, and I see a scar running down the left side of his face from under his hairline to the side of his mouth. Yep, I'm officially freaked out now.

Julian motions me to follow him up the stairs, and as I

do Mark falls in step behind me, uttering something about a kid dying in one of these last year. I shoot him a startled look and catch him grinning at Julian.

"Ok guys, you're real funny," I say to both of them without a hint of a smile on my face.

Julian laughs and says, "Yeah, I remember that. It was some girl with long brown hair, wasn't it?"

"You know, I think you're right," Mark says and gently nudges me to get me to walk through the dark open door in front of me.

We end up in some crazy room with all these white pieces of cloth hanging from the ceiling. To stay in line with the scary theme, they are playing one of those Halloween-type torture discs that have plenty of yelling, screaming, and loud machinery. A strobe light flashes from the ceiling. My nose starts to burn from the smell of dry ice that's being pumped onto the floor. I'm right behind Julian as we push our way through the cloth. It seems like it would be easy to lose someone in this sea of constant stimulation. The flashing is making me anxious, which I'm sure is its desired effect.

"I found the door!" Julian has to yell out in order for Mark and I to hear him over the sound of the chainsaw.

"Oh, wait, it's a door to nowhere."

We're all standing in front of this open black door revealing a painted black brick wall on the other side.

Julian walks along the wall checking all the doors we come to until he hits the jackpot. We go through the door, and instantly I feel as if I'm blind. Total darkness. I instinctively reach out and grab Julian's shirt so I'm not left behind. I'm not sure which is worse, constant flashing or extreme darkness. We just stand there for a second to let our eyes adjust. As they do, things start to come into focus.

"Oh man, this is messed up," Julian says, looking around.

I look back at Mark, feeling very uneasy now, and he

grabs my hand and smiles. "This is just a stupid fair fun-house, don't worry Jo."

I know this in my mind, but as I look around at all the disturbing images of death, dismemberment, and creepy clowns, I can't help but feel a little alarmed. Julian presses on through the room. We turn a corner and are back into a world of strobe lights. I stop and close my eyes, trying not to let the lights cause me to feel so disoriented.

When I open them again, I see that Julian has continued walking and is turning the next corner. Great, now we're separated. Just then one of those mechanical people dressed in a scary clown costume jumps out of the shadows and scares me. I jump back and scream. I cling to Mark as he lets out an uneasy laugh. As the mechanism puts the clown back into position for its next victim, Mark says, "I wasn't expecting that."

I stand there looking at that bizarre clown. Even though I know it's not real, it has an almost knowing expression on its face that makes it seem so eerie.

"I guess we lost Julian," Mark says as we start to walk along slowly toward the next turn. "Let's catch up to him," he says, and I realize I'm still clinging onto him, barely shuf-fling along.

"Sorry about that. I guess this place is better or worse than I thought it would be," I say, trying to smile.

"I know what you mean. It has some surprisingly realis-tic stuff."

We start walking again and go around the corner. Up ahead looks like more of the same, so I start moving faster just to get through it. My side is really starting to sting a bit, and when I reach down, my shirt is wet. I walk over to a white strobe light that's in the corner. Mark follows me.

"What's wrong?"

"I don't know. I think I might have gotten into

something," I say as I pull my shirt out away from my side to get a better look. I realize the whole side of my white shirt is now red. Mark sees it then, too, and quickly lifts it to check my side.

"Oh my God, Jo, you're cut."

"What . . . I am?"

Mark rips his shirt off then and presses the fabric against the wound. A shot of pain courses through my side as he applies pressure to it.

"Here, hold it in place like this," he says.

He picks me up and carries me in his arms as he makes his way quickly through the corridor of freakish images. It's as if he's on a mission and nothing is going to get in his way. I normally would be thrilled that he was holding me like this against his bare chest, but the pain in my side is making it hard to concentrate.

He walks into the next room and spots an exit sign. He quickly steps through the door and we realize we're behind the funhouse now. When we get to the front, he walks up to the creepy attendant man.

"Where's your first aid building?" he demands.

The man feebly stands up and points over to a place that looks like nothing more than a shack a few yards away. Seeing the man now, with Mark towering above him, makes him seem so small and weak. Nothing like he was before when I was feeling so skittish and creeped out.

Julian runs up beside us then as Mark is walking briskly toward the shack.

"What happened? What's going on?"

"Jo got cut. I'm taking her to the first aid station," Mark says in a matter-of-fact tone, still looking straight ahead stone-faced.

Julian doesn't say a word, just follows alongside.

It's not so bad inside the first aid station. It's just one

room that looks relatively clean and well lit. Maybe they make it look like a falling-down shack on the outside to go with the whole run-down theme for the funhouse.

An older woman dressed in scrubs sees us walk in and comes right over.

"What seems to be the problem?"

"She's been cut and is bleeding pretty bad," Mark says in a strained tone.

"All right son, bring her over here and lay her down so I can take a look."

Mark takes me over to a table, the kind you find in doctors' offices. I have a real knack for ruining a good time.

The nurse, or whatever she is, walks over to me and, seeing the amount of blood, curtly tells Mark and Julian to step back. I release my hand from Mark's shirt and pull it away from my side. She lifts my bloody shirt and sees the cut. "Oh my, you've got yourself quite a good cut here, haven't you?".

She takes a sterile pad and cleans some of the blood away from the cut.

"Well, that's interesting," she says. "You cut yourself, all right, but bled much more than I would have thought."

After cleaning it, she covers it with a bandage. "I was expecting it to be much deeper than it is, given. . . "

She stands up and stares at me for a minute. As I look up into her eyes, I can see lingering questions, but after a few seconds she just smiles and starts to put away the medical supplies.

"Well, it's strange all right, but you'll be fine. No need for stitches or anything."

As she starts cleaning up the bloodied bandages, she looks over at me and asks, "How did you hurt yourself?"

I tell her I don't know.

"What do you think could have cut her that way?" Mark asks.

"Well, I couldn't say. It's a lot of blood, though. I'm going to have to get your information for an incident report."

After filling out the paperwork, she tells us we can leave.

"Sorry about your shirt," I say to Mark.

"Hey, now I have an excuse to buy one of those cool carny T-shirts they sell here. Sahara will just love that," he says, giving me a knowing look.

I just smile and look away. I'm suddenly feeling awful about ruining his and Julians evening.

"Look, I'm going to call my dad to come get me," I say.

"Shut up dummy," Julian says. "I'm taking you home."

"Well, one good thing to come out of this. Now I'll have a good excuse to never step foot in another creepy funhouse," I say.

7

Heading downstairs to breakfast the next day, I contemplate how I'm going to tell my parents about my cut. I've been telling myself it wasn't a huge deal, but now as I'm formulating the words for my explanation in my head, I'm having doubts. Was someone trying to hurt me, kill me even? No, that's crazy. I'm just feeling paranoid because of the crap that's been going on lately. Regardless, I realize I can't tell my parents, they would freak.

In the kitchen, my dad is seated at the table with his face buried in a paper while my mom stands at the stove looking quite somber. That's weird, we don't get the paper. My parents get all their news from online sources.

They both look toward me when I walk in the room. "What's going on?" I ask, instantly feeling the strange vibe that's in the air.

My dad eyes my mom.

"There was another murder last night," he says, checking my reaction.

"Another murder?" I ask, letting the words sink in.

"Who was it? Where was it?" A part of me really doesn't want to hear the answers.

"It was a girl named Shelly-something from Weston High," he says, looking back at the paper.

Someone I didn't know.

"Where did it happen?"

My mom suddenly drops her spatula and looks away from me. My dad folds the corner of the paper down and says in a quiet voice, "At the fair last night."

On Monday, nobody at school seems to be talking very much about what happened in Mr. Geary's class last week. The whole thing died down quickly once word got around about the murder at the fair. It has the whole school freaked out. Although I haven't heard of anyone that knew her, I guess being at a place where a murder was committed was pretty hard for some kids to deal with.

Myself, hard doesn't begin to describe it. After leaving the kitchen in such a way as to not bring attention to my impending meltdown, Mark and Julian's calls finally convinced me that I wasn't an actual intended target. How knives or stabbing of any kind hasn't been the MO of the killer.

Just thinking about it now causes my pulse to quicken. I push away the thoughts that are starting to creep in my mind and focus on what I'm doing, getting books out of my locker for my next class.

Where is that damn book?

Everyone around me is buzzing. I overhear two girls at a locker down from mine talking about two new students. That must be what everyone is all worked up about. That's weird, though. I mean, we've had new students here before. I wonder why everyone is taking such an interest?

Listening to their conversation, I conclude that it's a brother and sister from some other town. I can't seem to find my Trig book in the giant pile in my locker. As I search through its contents, I hear a commotion coming from down the hallway. As it gets closer, I stop what I'm doing and look in its direction.

All I see is a crowd of students. Everyone peering down the hall trying to get a look. It reminds me of being at a concert right before the band finally comes out of a side door and makes their way to the stage. How everyone is doing anything humanly possible just to see them.

As the sea of students parts, I see two figures walking down the hall between them. How could two students possibly cause this kind of commotion?

Then I see them and know.

Walking toward me are the most incredible-looking people I've ever seen. I'm fixated.

The girl has long black hair. It sways slightly from side to side as she walks. Just enough to see the light reflect off each silky strand. Her tanned skin is flawless. She's a little taller than average with curves in all the right places. As she walks in my direction, only one word comes to mind. Seductress.

Then he comes into view.

Just as unbelievably attractive as the girl but contrasting her in every way. Sandy blond hair with a tan, sculpted physique. His movements are effortless and extremely charismatic. His chiseled features are perfectly proportioned. As he gets closer, I see he possesses magnetic grey blue eyes. The same eyes that are now looking my way. I'm frozen, mesmerized.

The girl eyes me up and down while the boy gives me a smile. They keep walking as I just stand there staring after them. All I can think is . . . these are high school students?

Later on as I walk in the lunchroom I notice right away how empty it is. I head over to my usual table and see Julian is already there. Sahara is standing next to him, busy saying something. He looks anything but happy. Today she has been uncharacteristically low-key, which is strange for her.

I walk up and sit down at the table. Sahara gives me her usual look of disdain. I ignore her and say, "Where is everyone today?"

In a voice riddled with irritation, Sahara says, "Since the new superstars are having lunch outside, I guess the rest of the student body has decided to follow suit. I honestly think it's absurd."

"I have to say, though, they're pretty much the best-looking new students to ever set foot in this school," I say, knowing full well she was a new student last year.

She just glowers at me then says, "I don't know about that. That new girl looks like a slut to me. I mean, do you have to openly check out every single guy you come across? It's like she's looking for her next victim or something."

"Yeah, maybe we should do some sort of undercover investigation. I mean, I'll volunteer to spend some time alone with her and then we can see if I live through it," Julian says lifting his eyebrows with a grin.

Sahara gives him a dirty look. "Real funny. Oh, and the brother and sister cover. I mean, really. He's about as related to her as I am to you," she says looking at me with complete contempt.

Mark walks up.

"Hey guys, pretty empty in here, huh?"

At the sound of his voice, Sahara lights up like a Christmas tree. "Oh, hey Mark," she says in the sweetest voice possible.

This girl knows exactly how to make my skin crawl.

Mark just looks at her, then looks at me and smiles. It's all so subtle, but am I picking up something in this interaction? I see right away that this little exchange wasn't missed by Sahara. She gives me the evil eye and makes some excuse and leaves.

Mark lets out a sigh and sits down. He seems relieved she's gone. That makes two of us.

"How about all this craziness with these new students?

It's nuts," Mark says.

I look at him and smile. "Yeah, I know. I guess if they're in the talent show, they can just stand there. I mean that's all they need to do to entertain the people around here."

"You're right," Mark says, giving me a warm look. "Oh Jo, I've been meaning to tell you. I know you usually ride with Julian but . . . I don't know . . . if you ever need a ride or anything I'd be more than happy to take you." He looks at Julian. "I didn't know if it was out of your way to come in our neighborhood."

Julian scowls at him and says, "It's never been out of my way before, but Jo may think otherwise now." Julian looks at me as if waiting for an answer. I just sit there, not sure how to respond.

Mark gives me a knowing look. "Well, I better go. I have some things to do before class. I'll um . . . see you around." Getting up, he smiles at me then leaves the lunchroom.

I know what's coming, and I can't think of any way to stop it.

"When did you two start getting so close?" Julian says looking at me accusingly.

"Mark probably just figures he'd be nice and offer to help you with your chauffeur duties. It's really not a big deal."

"Oh really, that's all there is to it, huh? I saw the way he looked at you. Give me a break, Jo. For years you lust after this guy, and he barely says hi, and now he's asking to be your personal driver and it's no big deal."

He looks away.

"I don't care that he has a thing for you now, and trust me . . . I can tell he does. I just really don't get it. You pretend we're friends but you don't open up about anything in your life. You go through all the motions but when push comes to shove. . . "

"Julian, I—"

"Forget it Jo. You know I noticed something going on between you two. I had just hoped that you'd be the one to fill me in, not him. What does that say about our friendship?"

What is it with Julian? It always seems like a tug of war between us, him wanting more from the friendship than I am willing to give. But I've never been able to put my finger on it—there's just something about Julian. Something that won't let me get close to him.

As we sit here in uncomfortable silence, I catch him looking at me. What's that look? Different. Strange.

"Look Jo, I'm sorry. You've been through a lot, and here I am causing you more problems," he says apologetically. "Listen, take Mark up on his offer. I mean this is your chance, right . . . so take it."

"Julian—"

"No really . . . and if things don't work out—I'll be waiting and ready to continue with my personal driving services," he says. "Just promise to fill me in on all the dirty details." He winks and nudges me.

I smile back but am still left with an uneasy feeling. I quickly push the feeling aside and remind myself that he's my friend, always will be.

That night I'm in my room trying to figure out the meaning behind a poem we're studying in English Lit. I never understand these things. I'm amazed what people can get from reading a few lines of what seems to me like nonsense. I'm supposed to find the deeper meaning. Heck, I can't even understand its literal meaning.

The doorbell rings. My parents went out tonight,

something about dinner with friends. I haven't eaten the dinner from the fridge my mom left. It's seven o'clock, and she'll kill me if I don't eat. Have I really been working on this stupid poem this long?

As I go to the front door, I can see through the glass that it's Mark. A jolt of electricity runs through me instantly as I reach out to open it.

"Hi."

"Hey, Jo."

I invite him in.

"Thank God you've come. You've saved me from English Lit hell," I say happily.

"Are you guys doing sonnets, too?"

"Yep, Shakespeare . . . ugh," I say and make like I'm stabbing myself with a knife.

He laughs.

"Do you want something to drink?" I ask and motion to go in the kitchen.

He takes my hand and, sounding serious, says, "No I'm fine. Listen Jo, I had to come over here. I'm really sorry about today in the lunchroom with Julian. I didn't know you and him. . . "

He doesn't think . . . oh great.

"No! No. We're just friends. I mean, it's not how it might have seemed. . . " I bite my bottom lip. How do I explain my relationship with Julian to Mark when I know it must have looked. . .

Mark's trying to read me. I have to tread carefully here.

"Julian and I have just been friends for a while, and ever since Aiden died I think he's been a little afraid that things may change between us. With the friendship and all. So when you offered to drive me, I think he just felt. . . "

I'm trying to explain it the best way I can, but I know

how it must look to Mark. Why is everything so complicated?

"Oh, well I just . . . I just want to help you. . . not cause you any trouble."

Was there some inner meaning in that statement?

He gives me a small smile. "Remember Jo, if you ever need anything, all you have to do is ask."

"Actually, could you do something for me?"

He gives me a serious look. "Of course, anything."

"Could you take me to school tomorrow?"

After he leaves, I keep thinking about what he said. Does he really think he might be messing up some romantic thing that Julian and I have? Or does he want to make it clear that he's here to help, but that's where his feelings for me end?

Just when I thought things were moving in the right direction. . .

As I lay there pondering all this, I start to feel a little hot. Then I feel my heart rate increase. Oh boy, here I go. . .

I'm out the window for another run.

Lacing up my shoes, I think about how much I'm looking forward to the final track meet today. It's been probably one of the worst days I've had in a while. Julian and Mark are both acting strange. And on top of that, I was off in all my classes, especially in English Lit. My interpretation of the poem was all wrong, and not just wrong, it really sucked.

I'm definitely in the mood to run today.

I walk out to the field and go up to Coach Miller to find out what race I'm running. His answer makes me smile. I'm on the relay race and I'm running the last leg. The fastest leg.

Our school is hosting this last meet of the season. I'm glad because it'll give us a home advantage. We'll need it. We're racing against three much faster schools.

Julian probably is the best runner for the boys' team, but he's not even participating today.

The relay race is last on the schedule. After a while of sitting here watching all the other races, I begin to feel antsy. I get up and jog around for a while just to clear my head. I'm feeling more agitated by the minute. Why can't Julian just chill? Why does he have to be so sensitive?

I'm lost in my thoughts when they call the runners over to line up for the relay race. The bleachers are full and people are walking around everywhere. It's so different from the practices. It seems like most of the school has come out to watch. Seeing all these people and knowing that the relay is always the most popular race of the meet gives me a rush. A surge of electricity seems to run though my body.

As we stand on the line, most of the runners are bouncing up and down. Moving all around to keep their muscles warm. The other three girls on my team seem comfortable with each other but are looking at me like they don't know what to think. I guess I'm the wild card, or maybe just the weird card. I don't care. They can think whatever they want, I just want to run. To race . . . to win.

I look over then at the girls from the other teams. All of them seem to have a particular look on their face. Determination.

All of a sudden I'm wondering if I should be out here right now. I'm not as good as these girls. What if those practice times were a fluke? Oh man, who am I kidding. I've gotten in way over my head, and now I'm going to let down my team and look like a complete fool.

The first four runners from each team line up. Our team is on the outside lane, seeing as we have the slowest times.

Each runner carries a baton that they'll pass to the next runner on their team after they have done their lap. As the organizer yells for them to get set, they all lean forward ready to take off at any second.

The gun goes off, and they're propelled forward as they start running. The whole place erupts into loud cheering, which causes a surge of adrenaline to course through my body. All the doubts that I have about my ability to perform are replaced by my need to compete. Each runner stays in their assigned lane as they move quickly around the track. As they come around the final bend for the first handoff, I can see our team is in fourth place.

Each runner hands her baton off to the next girl perfectly. The second leg is underway. As each girl passes the hundred-meter mark, she moves to the inside lane. From this vantage point I can see that our team has fallen a little more behind. The other three teams seem unbelievably fast. Their movements are fluid. The organizer of the race has now lined up each girl running the third leg in order of the runners coming in. As they come in for the handoff, the crowd goes wild. Again, the handoffs happen without a hitch.

As the next runner takes off around the track, I realize that the final leg of the race is next. The fastest, most important leg of the race . . . and I'm running it.

My team is still in last place and the team in front has extended their lead even more.

My mind is starting to wrap around exactly what I'm going to have to do to win this thing. The more I think about it, the more I can feel my body reacting. I know what my body is starting to do, and for the first time ever . . . I welcome it.

I've never felt like this before. I look at the girls I'm going to be running against. I size them up. My instincts are telling me that every one of them is my competitor. That I must and will beat them.

As the runners come in for the final handoff, the crowd starts roaring. Everyone screaming for their team. I can see my runner bringing up the rear. She has her eyes on me, as do the other girls from my team who have already run their leg of the race. Is that expectation I see on their faces? Hope, even?

My competitors do their handoffs and move out. I am the last runner waiting to receive her baton. Her ticket to start. Every second I stand there, the other runners get that much farther ahead. My teammate is coming in fast. Her eyes are locked on mine and for a second, just a split second, I know she sees it. She sees the look in my eyes. The look that tells her I'm about to kick ass.

I feel the cold metal in my hand. My feet react instantly. I feel an energy running through my body powering every muscle. I feel strong, fast, and hot. I'm focused on the first girl in front of me. I'm coming up on her fast. Very fast. I whip around her as if she's standing still. Then very quickly the second girl is right ahead of me. I pass her just as easily.

I see her then. The frontrunner. She has a big lead by now. She's going into the final turn. I'm moving up on her fast, but at this pace I'll never catch her. I need to go faster. Much faster. My body starts to react to my need.

I've never felt like this. So powerful. Am I even breathing? I'm coming up on her now. I'm getting closer. She's almost at the finish line. My muscles have a mind of their own. I'm moving so fast. I'm on top of her now . . . we've crossed the line.

It's over. We aren't running, just walking now. I'm not even out of breath. I can feel my heartbeat. Slow and steady. Something grabs my attention and I quickly look down my shirt at my chest. It's glowing. My entire chest is emitting some sort of light. I pull my shirt up high over my chest, hoping no one will notice, and start running to the locker room.

8

rankenstein.

I stare at the title of the book for the English Lit as-signment. I still can't believe it. When Mr. Geary passed out the papers earlier, I just sat there and thought, You've got to be kidding me. Of course it's Frankenstein. As the last bell for the day rings, I grab my books and head to my locker.

Although Julian and Mark both assure me that I haven't been the main topic of conversation ever since the whole track incident, I can't help feeling like a freak. Now this book assignment. How ironic.

Mark and I tried to figure out what exactly could be going on with me, spent hours Googling everything under the sun. Even went to the library and read some medical journals. Desperate, we finally left a message for some older guy that lives on the edge of town. Tom Perlow, a town football hero from years ago. It wasn't the fact that he went from a medio-cre player to school record breaker in a matter of months that caught our eye. No, it was the number of holes in his story. The vague answers he gave an interviewer for an article we stumbled across. Exactly the kinds of things I would say if I were in the same situation.

Grabbing the books out of my locker, I notice the stares and whispering are still going on. It's been like this all day, and frankly I'm getting sick of it. I decide to head to the library, thinking I can get a start on my reading assignment but mostly I just want to get away from everyone. I head down the hall and duck in. It's so quiet and peaceful in here.

This is exactly what I need.

I head over to a row of computers and am relieved to see that all the seats are empty. I go to the computer on the end and sit down. As I'm looking up information on Mary Shelley, someone sets their books down beside mine. I look up and am met with the most piercing black eyes I've ever seen. It's the new girl. She's standing there looking as if she just came off the runway from one of those New York fashion shows. Wearing a low-cut silky top with leathery black pants and knee-high, high-heeled black boots, nothing about her says high school. Her gorgeous black hair falls slightly past her lower back as she looks at me intensely with those dark eyes.

I'm suddenly feeling very self-conscious. Then she smiles. Not a warm friendly smile, but a smile nonetheless. She extends her hand to me, and I notice her perfectly manicured nails.

"Hi, we haven't met. My name's Giovanna, but I allow everyone to call me Gio."

I take her hand and shake it, feeling like the dowdiest girl that ever lived. "Hi, I'm Jo, well, I mean Josephine, but everyone calls me Jo," I manage to stammer out.

She glances over to the computer I was on.

"Working on something for class?"

"Oh, yeah, just researching something for my English Lit class."

Why do I get the feeling I'm being interrogated by this girl? Pointedly she asks, "How are you feeling? I heard about what happened at the track meet yesterday."

Ugh, here we go. I wondered why someone like her would seek me out. She must be one of those rumor-mill busybodies. I really don't have time for this.

She seems to read my reaction right away and puts her hand on my arm. "No, don't misinterpret why I'm asking.

I've had similar things happen to me before and . . . well, I know how mean people can be." How could she know what it's like to feel like a freak?

"It's not always easy to fit in when you're so. . . different," she says.

I'm pretty sure her idea of different is nothing like mine.

"But, sometimes being different makes you better," she goes on to say. "Think about it. I mean, after all . . . you did win the race."

She smiles and cocks her head to the side as if giving me a moment to digest what she just said.

"Josephine, I just know you and I are going to be great friends."

Then she walks away, leaving me feeling worse than I did before. Was she serious or is she just about the meanest person I've ever met?

I watch her saunter out of view then turn back to the computer, happy to be able to get back to the computer research.

I read about the author and Dr. Frankenstein. His creation is unnatural. He has no mother or father.

I think about my birth parents. My parents have always said they didn't know anything about them, so I don't either.

Did they know I had this condition, and that's why they didn't want me? Do I even have birth parents? Maybe I'm an unnatural creation.

I go on to read how this creation eventually turns into a monster. That the monster was made by his environment and experiences in life.

I think about what happened with Declan. What I was capable of on the track . . . the nightly episodes. Just like Frankenstein. Am I turning into some kind of monster or something?

I can feel tears stinging my eyes. I jump up and grab my

books. I have to get out of here. Get some air.

I leave the library and head down the hall.

I hear Mark call out, "Jo, hey, wait up." He's running up behind me. I'm in no mood to see him right now. I really just want to be alone.

As he comes up beside me, I just keep walking.

He gently grabs my arm. "Jo, hey, you all right?" I stop walking and look at him then. That beautiful face, so full of concern for me. For me, the monster. I'm the last thing he needs in his life right now. My craziness to add to his already complicated world.

"What's wrong?"

I can't look at him. All I want to do is throw my arms around him and never let go. Let him protect me from whatever is happening. Let him save me.

"It's nothing, just school stuff."

He looks at me doubtfully. "You sure you're ok?" he asks.

"Yeah, I just need to stay after and get some help with this English Lit assignment. So, guess I'll see you tomorrow?"

He's looks unsure.

"I can just hang around and wait. I mean, I have some things I probably need to do myself. . . "

"No!" I say loudly but then catch myself. "No really, you go ahead. I'll just see you tomorrow."

"All right, Jo," he says and gives me a slightly hurt look before walking off.

As I watch him walk away, my heart aches. Instantly I start doubting that pushing him away was the right thing to do. Am I just being selfish again? The tears start to flow as I head to the bathroom. When I get there, I burst through the door. Thank goodness nobody's here. I slide down the wall as the sobs come.

How can I possibly push Mark away? I wanted for so long to have him in my life and now that he is . . . I can't even think it. Can't even imagine it. No, I'll figure something out. I have too.

I stand up, looking in the mirror. I'm a little taken aback by what I see. All my typical imperfections are gone. My skin is the clearest it's ever been. My lips are full and moist with a slight rose color to them. My hair's normal dull brown sheen has been replaced a lustrous golden brown. When I reach up and touch it, I'm amazed at its softness. I pull a strand out and inspect it. But the biggest change is my eyes. They look like they have been transformed into two molten pools of amber-hued liquid. I'm mesmerized by them. I blink, thinking that I'm seeing things, but when I open my eyes I still see the same rich color staring back at me. So not only are things happening inside my body but obviously outside as well.

As I stand there taking it all in I suddenly hear someone coming in. Flustered, I grab my bag and books and rush out.

Next thing I know, I'm flying back as if I've run into a wall. I land on my butt, and my books go flying. I take a hand that's extended to me, and as I'm being helped up I find myself gazing into those stunning gray-blue eyes. I'm spellbound. He is the most perfect specimen of a human being I've ever seen. Every angle, every feature. Perfection.

"Hi, my name's Sandy," he says, never taking his eyes off of me. I'm transfixed. He looks down at our hands still clasped together. It seems to break the spell I'm under, and I immediately regain some of my senses. Chagrined, I laugh softly.

"I'm Jo."

"I know who you are, Josephine," he says matter-of-factly. He looks a little amused when I seem shocked by this. How could he possibly know me? Then it hits me . . . the dumb track meet. I lose my silly smile, and now I'm just embarrassed. I turn away from him and start gathering up my books. He bends down and helps me pick them up, all the while seemingly inspecting each one. What is it about these siblings?

"So are you late for something?"

"What?" I ask, not sure what he means. He motions to the door then and says, "Seemed like you were in a rush."

"Oh, the running-into-you thing," I say. "No, I guess I wasn't paying attention."

"Can I give you a ride home?"

I wonder why the heck he would ask that. Then he adds, "I noticed your boyfriend already left."

Taken a little aback I say, "Oh Mark, he's uh . . . "

"So do you need a ride?" he says and motions me to leave with him.

I'm unsure what to do, but then he flashes me the most charming smile. Seeing him standing there, looking at me that way, I'm unable to do anything but go with him.

We get to the parking lot, and I glance around at the cars. Most students have already gone home for the day, so there are only a few cars left in the lot. I spot a silver four-door Porsche and know immediately that's his car. What is it with these new students?

The car beeps as it's unlocked, and he opens the passenger door for me. I climb in and look around in awe at this car. I've never really cared much for this sort of thing but as I sit here, I really can't help but admire it. Sandy's the most charismatic person I've ever met and this car just seems like an extension of him.

The drive home is pretty chill. He's easy to talk to and seems interested in getting to know me. As he's pulling up to my house, I thank him and jump out.

I walk slowly up to the door. Then it hits me . . . I never told him where I lived.

So far, this day is just as crazy as yesterday. I absolutely hate the assignment in English Lit, and as I leave the class I'm feeling edgy. I'm at my locker when I hear that oh-so-familiar grating voice. There's Sahara standing with Mark at his locker. I straightaway feel a pang of jealousy.

They seem to be arguing, although I can't hear anything being said. He has his back to me, but I can tell by her expression that she's upset. I just stand there watching them, wondering what could be going on to make her so mad. All of a sudden she leans over, and her eyes lock with mine. Are they fighting about me? She turns her attention back to Mark, says something, and storms off. After a moment, Mark shuts his locker hard and heads in my direction.

I quickly start rifling through my locker so he doesn't know I was watching. I can tell he seems irritated but he smiles at me nonetheless.

"Hey Jo."

"Hey," I say, giving him a big smile. Trying to cheer him up without seeming to.

He seems to notice my better mood and perks up a bit. "Is your school stuff worked out from yesterday?"

"School stuff?" I ask and then promptly remember my excuse from yesterday. "Yes, all worked out."

He looks past me. I turn my head and see Gio leaning against the wall just watching us. How long has she been there? She slowly looks Mark up and down and then heads over. Right away I feel uneasy. This girl is so strange. Am I the only person that notices that there's just something about her that isn't right?

"Hi Josephine, going to introduce me to your friend?" she asks.

I'm quickly starting to get annoyed.

"Gio, this is Mark. Mark, this is Gio," I say curtly.

She holds out her hand to him and purrs, "It's actually Giovanna, but I guess you can call me Gio." As he takes her hand and shakes it, he's staring at her as if hypnotized.

I can't help but allow a small sound of disgust escape me as I watch this interchange. I mean, who shakes hands when they meet?

She turns to me then, dropping his hand like a lead weight, and says, "So Josephine, my brother drove you home yesterday, huh?" She winks at me and continues. "And I have to say, he was all smiles. If I didn't know better, I'd say he's interested in a certain track star we know."

Mark's looking at me now. Ignoring Gio, I turn toward him and manage to stammer, "Uh, I just needed a ride home and he was there. . . "

She interrupts me and looks at Mark.

"It was nice meeting you. Any friend of Josephine is a friend of mine." Then she turns, flipping her hair in such a way you can't help but notice how ravishing it is. "See you later, Josephine."

Mark's staring at the floor, and I can tell by his profile he's hurt, possibly angry. It looks bad and I feel awful.

"Mark, I really didn't—"

"Listen Jo, why didn't you just tell me you wanted to ride with him? I mean hell, you didn't have to make something up. What, you thought I wouldn't help you with your problems if you liked him? Jo, I'm your friend. I thought we at least had that."

He begins to walk off but stops, turns around, and adds, "You know, I'll make it easier for you. Just get a ride home with your new friend." Then he takes off down the hall.

9

Later as I sit at lunch, I stare at the door hoping that Mark will come in. I can't have him thinking what he does; it's eating me up inside.

Everyone at the table is talking about the talent show this Friday night. Julian is going on and on about the skit he and some other guys are doing. It sounds crazy, but until I resolve this thing with Mark I just can't concentrate on what they're saying.

I see people start to leave the lunchroom. Lunchtime is over. He never came in. Feeling dejected, I start to walk out but remember that I need to ask Julian for a ride home. Ugh, I really need to get a car of my own.

As the last bell rings, I sprint to my locker, hoping to catch Mark at his before he leaves. I wait around for a little while but then figure I must have missed him. I get the impression he must be avoiding me. This just makes me feel worse.

As Julian and I are leaving the school, he's still talking about that dumb talent show. He's in one of his great moods, which is making me feel more agitated. We get in his car, and as we pull away he asks, "By the way, I finished a new composition and was hoping you might want to come over to hear it."

"You sure you don't want to play one of your pieces for the talent show?" I ask knowing very well what his response will be.

"Honestly Jo, you know I'm not comfortable with these

goons seeing that side of me. I mean, heck, you're the only person I actually want to hear my music."

He just stares straight ahead as if lost in thought for a moment. Then he turns to me.

"How about it, wanna come over now?"

Of all times to ask me this. I haven't gone over there since before Aiden . . . ugh. It's the last thing in the world I want to do right now.

He looks at me, realizing that I'm not jumping at the chance.

"Jo, is there something wrong?"

I can feel the tears instantly spring forth.

"It's just that today isn't really a good day. I mean Mark and I had a disagreement. . . "

"Oh, I see. You and your boyfriend had it out, so here I am as usual at your beck and call. Just take me home but don't ask anything of me. Well, that's fine, Jo."

He reaches over and blasts the radio. I actually welcome the deafening sound. This is all becoming too much. "Julian, I'm so sorry. I didn't mean to hurt you."

"It's the story of your life, Jo," he says in an irritated tone.

When I get home he drives away without a word.

I head inside and straight up to my room. I throw myself on the bed and just lie there. I'm getting so sick of all the drama and misunderstandings.

After a while, I hear my dad downstairs. My mom's out of town, so I know I won't have to do the family dinner thing tonight. I'm in no mood. He's probably in his office already for the night. It seems like he's in there all the time now.

I sit there and stare at the computer for a while. Even though I've got to get going on my homework, I just feel so restless. Pulling my cell phone out of my pocket, I see it has a weak signal as usual. Of all times. . .

I get up and head downstairs, thinking maybe I should

try to call Mark. I hate not talking about things face to face but if he keeps avoiding me I have no choice.

I peek in my dad's office and see he's fallen asleep in front of the computer. Poor guy, this grant thing is wearing him out.

I go in the kitchen and pick up the phone. I dial Mark's number and wait. Finally, I get the answering machine. Ugh. I hang up without leaving a message. He's probably there but doesn't want to talk to me.

I'm sick of these boys and all their hang-ups. I grab my shoes, and as I'm headed out the door, I see my dad's car keys on the foyer table. I don't have my own car, so I hardly ever drive, but the thought of being behind the wheel and moving fast sounds like exactly the kind of therapy I need right now. Without another thought, I scoop them up and go.

My dad drives a Jeep SUV, which I think I've driven maybe a handful of times. It's so different from what I'm used to being in. It's big and sits really high off the road. I feel so small behind the wheel, but when my foot connects with the gas I feel its power. I take off and leave my neighborhood, knowing exactly where I want to go.

I'm headed to the edge of town where the mountain ridge starts. There's a two-lane road up there that winds around as you head up the first mountain. I just want to drive, and drive fast.

Thoughts of the day pop in my head. I could never hurt Mark. How could he even think I would purposely mislead him like that? I think I've made it clear how I feel about him with some of my past actions. Does he not see it? Do I really have to spell it out for him? Realizing my mind is straying within my own thoughts, I try to focus back on my driving.

Heading through town, I'm getting used to the feel of the Jeep. I'm loving the way I'm in control.

I can see the edge of the ridge now. Once I go through

this last light, I'll be on the two-lane and I can really see what this baby can do.

I hit the gas when the light changes. The engine responds at once. I take the first curve and easily maneuver through it. Not thinking about anything else, my mind is totally in the moment.

Through every curve the Jeep handles with ease. I pick up speed and go faster on every straightaway, getting braver and more fearless every minute. The curves are getting sharper as I go higher. Higher and faster.

In the distance I notice the curve ahead is different, sharper. That's when I see a sign. I know what the sign is probably trying to tell me. Why else would it be here? I don't care. It that means you better slow down if you want to live.

Then fear, logic, who knows, pushes its way back into my brain. I react, pushing hard on the brakes to slow down and stop completely. I throw the gear in park. Breathing heavily, a little laugh escapes me as I look to the side and realize I was teetering on the edge of the mountain. I sit there on the edge of the road and just put my head back against the headrest. Closing my eyes I feel the pounding in my chest slow back to a steady rhythm.

I feel exhilarated. I sit back up and put the gear into drive. I turn the Jeep around to head back down toward home.

I take the curves slower on the way down. Having gotten whatever that was out of my system, I'm just enjoying being out here.

Seeing headlights up ahead, I realize they seem to be coming at me fast. Someone get the same idea I did?

The car passes by me going faster than I would ever attempt. Now that's just plain crazy, I think as I continue down the winding road at a reasonable speed. Out of nowhere the car comes up behind me, trying to pass on the right. I slow way down to let it, but it just continues to drive next to me not passing. I'm starting to get a little freaked out, especially when I look over and it's this all-black car with dark windows that I can't see into.

I speed up, trying to get away. I'm going much faster around the curves, but the car stays right behind me. It's so close that if I slammed on the brakes, it would surely hit me. I take the next curve a little too fast, and the Jeep slides a little on some loose dirt, taking my breath away. Suddenly I'm feeling much less in control.

What the hell could this person want? Are they just messing with me, or am I really in some sort of danger?

Fine, you want to follow me. . .

I push on the gas and feel the Jeep accelerate, challenging this person to follow. They don't back down. I can see the light up ahead, which means the end of the two-lane. The light's green, so I pick up speed. If I can just make it to town, maybe I can lose them.

I blaze through the light, but the road is different. I hit a bump going too fast and swerve off the edge onto the embankment on the side. The Jeep skids around, and I lose control for just a split second. But it's a second too long. I'm headed into the trees.

The Jeep just barely clips the first one, sending me sideways toward another one. This can't be happening.

I smash into the tree.

When the Jeep shudders and stalls, I'm still unable to grasp what's just happened. The passenger-side window is broken. The front windshield is cracked, too. My head is killing me. Leaning forward against the steering wheel, I feel something run down my face. I reach up to wipe it away, and when I bring my hand down I see something red on my fingers. It takes a minute for my brain to register what I'm seeing.

I'm starting to feel a little lightheaded and tingly. I fumble around and pull my phone out of my pocket. With shaking fingers, I look down at the numbers and dial. . .

"Well, if you remember anything else, give us a call," the cop says and hands me his card.

"You folks have a good night and drive safe." Then he's gone, stepping through the hospital door.

I look over at my dad. All I can think about is how sorry I am. I feebly smile at him, and he pats my head.

"You ready to go home?"

"You have no idea," I say as I start to get up.

Reaching up, I run my fingers over the big bandage that's on my head. They said it's a good-sized gash, but otherwise I'm just banged up a little. One thing I do know: I have a killer headache.

"You all right, Josie?" my dad says. I give him a reassuring smile and nod.

As we're walking out of the hospital, he says, "I called your mom, and she wants you to call her when you get home." I just sigh.

I cringe as we get into my mom's Volvo. It's weird seeing my dad drive it.

"Dad, I feel terrible about the Jeep."

He doesn't say anything, just drives and looks ahead. I really messed up.

"Josie, what's going on with you?"

"I don't know . . . I guess I just feel like everything is out of control lately."

He just sits there and doesn't respond for the a few

minutes. When I glance over, it's hard to read his expression. This is all new territory for us. I've never really been in trouble before.

"Josie, I know . . . I know it's been hard for you lately. You had a really terrible thing happen, with Aiden and all. It's just you . . . you have to think before you act. I mean, listen, life's changing for you . . . changed for you, and your mom and I are worried." He lets out a big sigh and then looks over at me.

As the tears start to run down my face all I can think of is how sorry I am. Sorry that I reacted without thinking of how it might affect him. Like Julian said, it's been the story of my life lately.

"I really am so sorry, Dad," I say through the tears.

"I know you are," he says and pats my hand.

"We'll get through this. How about we chalk this one up to one of those life lessons. A big life lesson," he says then laughs a little.

Right away feel the tension leave my body and my mood lift. We smile at each other, and a small glimmer of happiness creeps back into my consciousness. We're all right again.

When we get home, I start to head upstairs and then remember my mom. I look at my dad and figure it's worth a try. "Dad, I'm feeling really tired and my head hurts. Could you just hold off mom until the morning?"

He sizes me up and then says with an inkling of humor in his eyes, "Sure Josie, you go on to bed and stay home from school tomorrow if you need to." I head up and can't help feeling like I just received a stay of execution.

Sitting up in bed suddenly, I realize I'm shaking all over. It takes me a minute to recognize my surroundings. Ok . . . I'm in my room. I see sunlight coming in through the curtains. Late morning sunlight. I lie back again and just stare up at the ceiling.

Thank God, it was a dream. Just a dream.

I've heard of people that have dreams so vivid and seemingly real that they think they must be premonitions. It was just too real. It has to mean something.

My head is throbbing, but the rest of my body seems fine from the accident. The accident. Did that really happen last night? I wish that had been a dream. I feel so stupid. How could I have been so reckless? I think of my parents then and hate that I've caused them to have to worry about me. How can they not? I have been acting a little off lately, and now this. . .

I decide I'm in no mood to go to school today. I need time to think, to sort out my feelings about Mark. The dream pops into my head again, and the details flood back.

I'm sitting in the back seat of my dad's Jeep. I look toward the front and see that Sandy is driving and Gio is in the front passenger seat. I don't know why I'm there so I keep trying to ask them, to get their attention, but they don't hear me. It's as if they don't know I'm there.

Then I realize Mark is sitting next to me on my right. He's staring out the window while holding a picture of his dad. He doesn't know I'm there, either. They pull up to a building and Mark gets out, closing the door behind him. It's the university my dad works for. Is he going to college? Why is he here?

Just then the black car from my accident is there pulling up next to Mark. I try to get out of the Jeep. To warn him. To help him, but I can't. The door won't open. All I can do is sit there and watch. He just stands there looking at the building as the black car idles next to him. It's as if he's contemplating something. He looks over at the car and then gets in the driver's seat. I see that nobody's in there as he climbs in and closes the door. I start beating on the window, yelling for him to get out. Sandy and Gio don't react. Sandy finally drives off, leaving Mark in that black car all alone. I'm yelling at him to stop. To go back . . . not to leave. They are totally ignoring me. I look back just in time to see the black car burst into flames. I start frantically beating on the window. I try to grab Sandy, but I'm unable to reach him. I look back then and the car's gone. . .

What the hell was that? I've never had such a crazy dream.

Even though it isn't real, I just can't bear to think about it. How could I? Even the remote possibility that something like that could happen is enough to. . .

I jump out of bed and head for the bathroom. The cut on my head instantly sends me a little reminder of its existence. I instinctively reach up and touch the bandage. I guess I better change it.

I spend the rest of the day mulling over things in my head. The talent show is tonight and I know I'm going to see Mark and Julian. I need to talk to them, to make things right. Plus, Julian would kill me if I missed his skit.

10

—

s we pull into the school parking lot, I'm astounded by how many people are here tonight. Cars are everywhere. I know this is a popular event, but I had no idea that this year it was going to be so big. I guess the student committee in charge of promoting it really did their jobs.

My dad pulls the car to the front and puts the gear in park.

"You sure you're feeling up to going tonight?"

I wasn't, not by a long shot, but I couldn't let him know that.

"I'm fine dad . . . really. My head doesn't hurt anymore, and I got plenty of rest today."

"Call me when you need me to come get you. And Josie. . ." He has a serious look on his face and starts to say something but then stops and decides not to. "Just have a good time."

"Thanks dad, and really, don't worry," I say and give him a big grin.

As I walk into the school, I can hear the loud, booming of music coming from the auditorium. I'm running late, and the show has already started. I know that Julian and Mark both have their skits toward the end, so I'm not worried about missing them. I walk up to the long table that's set up outside the auditorium doors. Two girls, part of the planning committee, are collecting money and tickets to get into the show. I give them my money, and they ask about my head. After telling them a lame story about running into something, I make my way to the closed doors. I pause to collect my thoughts for a moment. I always feel like a fish out of water with these school functions anyway, but tonight it's more than that. I've planned out in my mind what I want to say to Mark. After the show I'll just ask to speak to him a minute and then. . .

The auditorium has been transformed into what looks like a dark, loud, raucous concert. The entire place is packed with people hooting and hollering as a group of seven students are on the stage doing a dancing and singing act. They're pretty good, and I stand there in the back of the auditorium and watch them perform. They all have on white shirts with jeans and are singing a rendition of some popular pop song. My mood lifts, and I'm suddenly glad I came.

I glance around the room and begin to appreciate all the work that must have gone into putting this show together. Draped along the back of the stage is a billowy velvet jet-black curtain. The whole stage is lit up with an array of bright lights as the students dance all around. Looking in the direction of where the lights are coming from, I see a boy there controlling what must be some sort of light machine. I look back at the stage as the act is ending, and the entire auditorium erupts in screaming and applause.

A boy named Daniel from drama club comes out on the stage. He's always been one of those outgoing people who thrives on attention. Just being around him always wears me out. He's wearing a really tall black top hat with a tux. He goes on to say something funny. The audience cheers.

I'm still just standing in the back when the next act starts, a kid doing a guitar solo. I drown out the so-called music and look around for Mark or Julian. It's so dark in here that I'm having a hard time seeing. I make my way along the side of the auditorium, looking down each row for a familiar face. When I get to the first row, I see an empty seat right in front of the stage. Perfect, I think, and head toward it. As I sit down the guitarist finishes his number, and a group of what must be his entourage starts yelling his name and acting obnoxious.

Daniel comes out on stage and tells a joke just as I spot Julian standing by the exit door. He seems to be searching the audience for someone. He's probably looking to see that I made it here. Looking to see that I didn't find another way to drop the ball on our friendship. I raise my hand a little to get his attention and he sees me. At first he just looks at me, surprised, then gives me a faint smile. It's odd, his reaction. Maybe he's just having some last-minute nerves before having to go on stage.

When the lights go out, the music starts for the next act. A spotlight is illuminated on the stage, and I see a girl standing in the middle of it. The entire auditorium is silent. Everyone is looking at this girl, waiting for her to start singing. She looks too young to be a high school student, and I don't remember ever seeing her before. It wouldn't be impossible, though, given that our school is one of the largest in the city.

She's wearing a beautiful full-length black dress and seems extremely nervous. Her hair, which looks like spun gold, is pulled back into some sort of braid. She seems so small, but it could just be the way she's acting. I can see that she's scared to death as she just stares out, eyes fixed on the wall straight ahead. As the music goes on, she misses her mark to start. She's frozen. When the music stops no one makes a sound, and it takes only a few seconds for the music to start again from the beginning. By her vacant stare, I don't believe she's going to make her mark again. Feeling sorry for her, I want to help in some way. I instinctively stand up to get her attention. Since I'm in the first row, it works, and her eyes fly to me. I give her my most reassuring smile and keep standing until she begins to sing . . . right on cue.

Her voice is astonishing. I'm completely overwhelmed by how moving it is. And to think she was nervous. Her eyes never leave mine for a moment. It's as if she's drawing every ounce of her courage from me. And I'm willing to give it. The audience and I sit transfixed. I don't breathe as she holds the last note out with the precision of an expert. When her song's over, the entire audience stands, applauding enthusiastically. Everyone seems just as amazed as I am by her talent. She bows, smiling sweetly, and then looks at me and mouths the words thank you.

Daniel comes back on the stage again as I start looking around for Mark. Just thinking about him gets the butterflies going in my stomach. I want to talk to him, to tell him exactly how I feel, but once I do I know there's no going back. Part of me wants to just forget the whole thing. To just apologize for being a lousy friend and then say something witty and go on with the way things have been. It would be so easy. But what is it they say—nothing worth anything is easy. Something like that sounds good anyway.

When the next act starts, it's a band playing one of my favorite songs. As I sit here thinking how surprised I am at the amount of talent some of these students have, I see him. He's backstage. Seeing me he smiles. Watching him standing there, with this song playing, does something to me. At that moment I can't wait any longer. I'm impulsively drawn to him. I have to talk to him, now. . .

I stand up and quickly head to the stairs on the side of the stage. These should take me back behind it. I'm not sure exactly where I'm going and it's dark, but the music mixed with my emotions drives me on. Once I get to the top, I head down a short, narrow hall that brings me to a large open space.

It's very dark but I can see there are only a few students crowded over by the edge of the open stage, watching the band. The music floods the entire area. I'm there standing beside him then. I touch his arm to get his attention. He turns around and looks surprised when he sees me. His eyes tell me that he's glad to see me, but then they move up to my head.

"Jo . . . what happened?" he asks loudly so I can hear him over the music.

I instinctively reach up and touch my bandage. Great, this adds a certain elegance to the whole moment.

"Mark, can I talk to you for a minute?" I mouth and then I motion for him to follow me over to a corner that's vacant and dark. Privacy is a necessity at this moment.

He nods and gives me a confused look but follows.

When we get to the corner, the noise level has dropped back down into a somewhat normal range. At least I won't have to scream what I have to say at him. He gently grabs my arm. "Are you all right . . . what happened?"

He's searching my face for some indication of my condition. He really does look worried. Should I take his concern personally or is it just Mark being the naturally caring person that he is?

"Jo?"

As I stare into those eyes, that face, I can't find the words. The words that I've gone over so many times in my head. I knew this was going to be hard, but my thoughts are just blank. I'm frozen in indecision. Part of me wants to turn and run and another just wants to cry. It's as if all the years of thinking and hoping about him have come to a head.

I can tell he's really starting to get worried. I must look like a crazy person. I have to say something. Do something.

"I know this is a strange time and place, but I need to tell you something. I just can't wait any longer."

He's just looking at me, waiting. He doesn't seem to have any idea what I'm about to say. He's just staring at me with that same concerned look in his eyes.

"Mark, I know that lately I've acted like a lousy friend. . ."

"Jo, don't worry about it. I'm not mad or. . ."

"I love you," I say abruptly as tears start to run down my face. I study his expression for any inclination of what he might be thinking.

Before I'm able to even think about what I'm saying, a whole stream of words pours out.

"I've loved you for so long. Longer than you could even know. Longer than I probably should have."

He's just staring at me, not saying a word. What's he thinking? He's probably thinking of a way to get out of this crazy situation, away from this lunatic.

"I'm sorry Mark . . . I just had to tell you. I couldn't keep going on like we were, without telling you how I really feel."

My cheeks are wet. I look down, racking my brain, trying to figure out a way to backpedal a little, to make this situation more comfortable for us both.

I look up at him and see that his expression has changed. Suddenly embarrassed, I feebly apologize, but he stops me from talking with his finger over my lips. He takes my head in his hands and just stares into my eyes so intensely that it takes my breath away. I see now what the difference is in his look and my heart instantly starts beating quicker. I'm not breathing, not moving. I'm frozen in his gaze as his head bends toward me. I instinctually close my eyes as his lips find mine. So gently at first but then immediately deepening. I throw my arms around his neck as he lifts me up and leans against the wall that's behind me. I wrap my legs around his waist as we kiss, more frantic now. Both wanting to do more than we could possibly do backstage in the high school auditorium.

"Julian, get over here, you're on next," I hear a girl yell in our direction. It instantly breaks our moment. We pull away from each other, looking in the direction of the girl's voice, and I see someone quickly leave the area. It's dark so I can't be sure, but a part of me is afraid I know exactly who it was.

Mark and I smile at each other and then he hugs me. A tight hug that makes me feel safe and loved. Connected to him on the best level possible. We stay like that through the next two acts, just hugging each other and taking it all in.

He pulls away and looks at me. He looks happy, and I know I am.

"Do you need a ride home tonight?" he asks, smiling at me sweetly.

"From you . . . always." I say with a knowing expression on my face.

Laughing, he leans over and brushes his lips gently across mine.

"Meet you out front after the show."

Then he heads to the side of the stage just as Daniel is announcing his act. I watch as he runs on stage along with five other guys, and they start their performance.

I watch as they act out an impression of one of our teachers. The crowd is laughing and going wild, but all I can think of is how happy I am. As I stand there watching the skit, I have a huge grin on my face. I've never felt happier. Ever.

After the show, I walk outside to wait for him. I sit down on a bench and watch as all the students pile out of the school in an excited frenzy. There's a lot of hooting and hollering going on as they start hop in their cars and driving away. I'm enjoying watching when I spot Julian headed toward me.

My stomach churns in anticipation of what's to come.

Did he see us? I shift uncomfortably in my seat as he gets closer. When he sees me, his reaction throws me off guard. He shoots me a smile as he heads over and sits down next to me on the bench.

"So what did you think?"

It takes me a couple of seconds to realize he's talking about his act.

"Oh . . . you were good," I say sheepishly realizing I missed his act entirely.

"Did you catch my joke about Mr. Edwards?" he asks, now eyeing me oddly.

"I . . . uh," I stammer.

He stands up abruptly. "Well, they knew what they were getting when they signed me on," he says.

Guilt courses through me.

"Well, gotta run. I'm taking Taylor out for a celebratory . . . well, you know. . . " And then he walks off, only turning around for a moment to throw me an odd look and to say a quick "By the way, thanks for coming Jo."

I watch him walk away, thinking how yet again I dropped the ball on our friendship. But why didn't he call me on it? It's not like him not to say anything. It would have been better if he had just let me have it. I mean, I have more practice dealing with that.

I look over then and see my dad drive up to the curb and park. Why is he here? It's to be expected, I guess, with the accident and all. This newfound doting is definitely going to mess up my lifestyle, I think as I walk over to the car.

"Hey, Dad. I didn't know you were coming back to get me?"

"I know we left it up in the air, but I figured I'd stop by just in case," he says, giving me shrug.

"I guess you don't need that ride after all," I hear Mark say as he walks up behind me.

At that moment I realize how having busy parents is a good thing.

"Sorry," I say, giving him a shrug.

Mark leans through the open window to say hi to my dad and then helps me into the car. As he shuts the door, he says with a wink, "I'm really glad you came tonight." Then he stands up, and my dad drives away leaving him staring after us.

"How was the show?"

I smile to myself and say, "The best talent show I've ever seen."

Later that night as I stand in front of the bathroom mirror, my mind keeps thinking back to our kiss. It was everything I could have wished for. Everything I ever wanted a kiss with Mark to be like. My body reacts instantly at the possibilities.

Needing to change my bandage, I reach up and take it off. My head is smooth and flawless. I stare at the place where just this morning there was a gash, but now it's completely gone. I look closer in the mirror but don't see a thing, no sign that I was ever even cut. Not even a slight scratch. Nothing.

How can this be, I think now, rubbing my fingers along the area hoping to feel something. A rough patch. A dip in the skin. Anything.

I reach down and splash water on my face. When I look in the mirror again all I see are tiny drops of liquid streaming down my forehead. As I stand in the shower letting the hot water run all over my body, I try to figure out how I could have healed so quickly. I think back on other times that I've hurt myself, and the only other injury that stands out in my mind is the cut I got at the fair. That was a pretty weird injury, but this. . .

After showering off, I go to my room and get on the computer. As I'm looking up information on healing, Julian pops in my mind. He never even asked me about my head. I figure he probably did see Mark and I together backstage, but wouldn't he still at least ask what happened to my head?

I push my thoughts of Julian away when articles come on the screen about people with the ability to heal quicker than others. Everything I read talks about how you can take these new scientifically formulated drugs to help promote the healing process. Even with these drugs, though, nobody would ever be expected to heal as quickly as I did. In other words, I have nothing. Again, there's no reasonable explanation for the odd things that are happening to me.

11

—

The next day it's Saturday and I'm back on the computer trying to figure out what's going on with my body. I've been at it all morning, but nothing I read seems to make sense. Still frustrated, I turn the computer off and head downstairs. Although I no longer have a gash on my head, I'm wearing a bandage. There's no way of explaining this to my parents that won't freak them out.

They are both in the office bent over the computer intently staring at the screen when I walk in.

"Hey, anything going on today?" I ask seemingly surprising them both.

"Hi honey, just helping your dad sort through this tedious research. How's your head?"

"Oh, it's much better. Just cleaned it and changed the bandage. Should be healed in no time," I say without making eye contact.

My dad, still staring at the screen, is typing away at his usual incredibly fast pace.

"Good . . . well, by the looks of this mess I may have to go with your dad to his office today to help him get a head start on this research compilation," she says and glances over at him. "There's leftovers in the fridge or we can bring you dinner, but it might be on the later side."

"Leftovers are fine, mom. Don't worry about me, just go help dad with the research comp . . . whatever it is," I say, giving my best reassuring smile.

"All right honey, just call us if you need anything," she

says, already looking back at the screen.

I walk in the kitchen and grab some chips and a Coke. Everything is perfectly in its place. Even with my parents right there in the office, our house is quiet. It always is. With me in my room and my parents in the office, I think of all the other rooms that nobody hardly ever enters. Rooms that are never used. Just like one of those model homes.

I think of Mark's house. Comfortable and cozy. Sounds of laughter, TV, talking . . . whatever, just sounds. Proof that someone is living there.

As if on cue, I hear my cell phone ringing upstairs and run to get it.

Deciding not to wear the bandage, I have just finished brushing my hair when the doorbell rings. My heart skips a beat. Mark had called earlier and we made plans for him to come over. My parents are still at the office. This is the first time we'll be alone since I avowed my love for him. I give myself one last once-over before heading down.

When I open the door he's standing there with a freshly picked flower. He's wearing a tight gray long-sleeved shirt that clings to every muscle in his arms. His dark hair is purposefully tousled above his beautiful brown eyes, eyes that are smiling down at me right now as he holds out the flower.

"Thank you."

He comes in and I close the door. For a few seconds we just stand there, not sure what to do next. I usually feel so at ease with him, but this is uncharted territory. How do I act, like a girlfriend?

"Do you want anything to drink?" I finally ask.

"No, I'm fine, thanks," he says and gives me a look like he's just as uncomfortable as I am right now.

"You wanna . . . go upstairs?"

"Yes, I mean . . . sure," he slightly stammers.

I head upstairs with him close on my heels. I feel like one of those girls from the old time brothels that takes the guy up to a chosen room to earn her living. And after what happened between us at the talent show, I'm not sure what my expectations should be.

As we head to my room, my heart rate begins to increase, and I'm starting to feel a little hot. I'm instantly reminded of what happened the last time we were in there alone together. As we enter the room, I try to focus on a random drawing on the wall. Anything to distract my thoughts. I mean, how many times can I attack him and still expect him to be so understanding?

He walks over to a picture I have on my dresser of my parents together when they were younger. Many years before I came along.

I follow him over, now feeling much more like myself.

"Wow, your parents look so young."

"Yeah, that was right after they got married. This is my favorite picture of them . . . I always thought they looked so in love here," I say as I gaze down at their smiling faces.

I look up and catch Mark staring at me. Our eyes lock and he reaches over to brush a loose piece of hair away from my face. He runs his fingers through it. I'm spellbound as I watch him gaze over my hair and then look back to my face. Cradling my head in his hands, he tilts my chin up.

"You're so beautiful," he whispers to me as his head lowers. My eyes close as his lips softly graze mine, lingering for a few seconds before finding their mark. His kiss deepens ever so slightly. It's a kiss filled with the promise of love. A tender kiss.

I feel my heartbeat . . . nice and steady.

He pulls away and looks into my eyes for a moment. He's staring . . . searching. For what? He smiles and straightens up. I smile back, and then we both chuckle a little.

He continues on with his exploration of my room and its contents. I mechanically answer all his questions, but feel as though we are both unsure what to do next. Our relationship has taken a huge leap forward, and I think our minds are trying to play catch up.

We spend the next couple of hours just sitting on my bed talking. Not talking about anything in particular, just talking . . . hanging out and enjoying each other's company. I love the way everything can be so easy with him.

After he leaves, I go back to my room and lie on the bed. I run back through the entire night in my head. Him lying on his side, head propped up by his arm, smiling at me. The way he would touch my hand as he listened to me drone on and on about my life. How interested he was in knowing everything about me. Laughing as I tell him about my goofy childhood antics.

The way my heart would skip a beat when I would catch him staring at me with a wanting expression on his face. I fall asleep dreaming of him.

My breathing is shallow, if I'm even breathing at all. My entire body is on fire. As his lips find mine, a groan escapes from deep in his throat. The sound threatens to send me over the edge. I throw my head back as he kisses my neck, making my skin burn with every touch. I'm pinned up against the wall, his body against mine in such a way his longing for me is evident. His breathing has grown shallow, and when he whispers my name it sends a shudder through me. Every touch, every kiss, causes us to become more desperate. My entire body screams with anticipation as the fire within me rages.

My eyes fly open as the manic images of our lovemaking flash through my mind. My breathing comes out in short spurts. I jump out of bed too fast and stumble to the ground. When I regain some semblance of balance, I'm able to push myself to my feet. My eyes focus on my surroundings. I'm in my room . . . alone. It was a dream?

My heart is racing. I can feel the heat radiating throughout my body. I'm in a full-blown episode, and by the way I feel, this is a bad one. I frantically throw on my shoes and slam open the window. I don't have time to deal with the tree. I just jump. Jump right out of the window, landing perfectly on the ground. I'm off . . . running in a full sprint. I have to get to the water, to run to it. My body feels like it's on fire, and I have to put it out. Have to get to the water. As I run, the light around me gets brighter. I'm feeling hotter, more focused. Houses, yards are going by so fast.

I see the fence up ahead. It's looming around the house like a great wall. I'm up to it now, and before I even realize what I'm doing, I'm leaping over it. I land gracefully on the other side. I see the water then. The large swimming pool glistening as it's illuminated by the underwater lighting. I reach it in less than a second, diving into its cool refreshing water. I stay there for a while, under the water, feeling my body cool down and my heart rate slow. It's so cool . . . so calm under here.

I'm under the water for far too long. Am I even holding my breath? Startled by the thought, I shoot to the surface. I breathe in but not frantically, not as a person should who's been underwater that long.

I swim over to the stairs. As I drudgingly climb out of the pool, I look down at my dripping clothes and see that I'm glowing. My entire chest is radiating some sort of light. It's shining right through my wet, clinging shirt. When I'm finally out of the pool, I drop to my hand and knees. I'm exhausted, completely spent.

I feel the tears start to sting my eyes. Pushing them back, I roll over on my back. I feel the roughness of the cool river rock deck underneath me. I just lie there for a few minutes, looking up at the sky and breathing. I hear the steady hum of the pool filter and the gurgling sounds of moving water. I concentrate on these sounds, keeping my mind blank.

I look down at my chest and see that the glowing light has almost completely ebbed out. I reach under my shirt and feel the heat of my skin. My chest is so hot that the front of my shirt is warm and drying faster than the rest of my clothes.

My heart rate is slow and steady now. I sit up and look around. I know exactly where I am. This is the Andersons' house. I used to babysit for them when I was younger. They live in a gigantic house with one of the only swimming pools in our neighborhood. I used to love to come over here. I would take the kids swimming in the pool and have such a good time that I always felt guilty taking their money afterward.

I could understand wanting to come here if I were looking for an escape. But the one thing I can't wrap my head around is how I got here so quickly. They live over five miles away from me.

All the lights are still off in the house. I can't believe I didn't wake anyone up. Must be out of town, I think thankfully.

I stand up and my legs feel wobbly and sore. I really did run all this way. I walk over to the gate and realize it's padlocked. I look up at the fence. It's at least fifteen feet tall.

How did I jump over that?

I walk over to the pool and grab a lawn chair. I take the chair over to the fence and, using that and a strategically placed planter, I hoist myself up to the top ledge of the fence. I sit on the top and look down the other side. It seems too far to jump. I look around for another way down, but there's nothing on that side of the fence to help me. Probably to keep people from coming in, I guess.

All I can do is jump and hope I land ok.

No such luck. When I land on the sidewalk below, my legs immediately buckle and I fall on my hands and knees. Pain shooting through them, I just stay there for a minute before slowly getting up. As I start to make the over five-mile hike back home, my hands and knees stinging, I finally break down and start crying.

These episodes are definitely getting worse.

I wake up to my cell phone ringing. It takes a couple of seconds for my mind to register where the sound is coming from. I get up out of bed and grab it off my desk. As I answer it I throw myself back into the warm softness of my comforter.

"Hello," I say in a somewhat groggy voice.

"Hey sleepyhead," I hear Mark say on the other end.

"Oh, hey. What time is it?"

"Let's just say after sitting out front for a few minutes, I decided I better come to the door to get. . . "

"Oh my god, I overslept!" I say looking at my phone. "I'll be right there!" I run downstairs and open the door not even contemplating what I look like. I see Mark standing there looking as handsome as usual with a huge grin on his face.

"Let me just grab some clothes."

I run upstairs and head straight to the bathroom. Thank goodness I always sleep in shorts and a T-shirt. Got to be ready for those nightly runs. Then I think about last night. It all comes flooding back, and I remember why I'm feeling so tired and sore this morning.

My parents are both long gone by now. It seems they've both been going into work earlier these days. And staying later for that matter.

I hurriedly brush my teeth and throw on a little makeup. With my skin looking so much better lately, I barely have to wear any at all. I hurry to my room to throw on some clothes. When I get there, Mark is lying on his side on my bed with that same grin on his face.

"I'm so sorry to make us late," I say as I open my closet and grab anything that looks remotely fashionable.

"Honestly, if I could sit here and watch you get ready every morning, I'd be willing to be late everyday."

"Oh, would you?" I say and throw a pillow at him that had fallen on the floor when I bounded out of bed.

He laughs, and at that moment I know that if I could wake up everyday for the rest of my life and have him with me, I would be completely and utterly content.

At school everybody's talking about the talent show. I have to say it's nice for a change to be able to take part in a school-related conversation. To feel a little like I fit in. As I stand at my locker, my thoughts shift to the episode I had last night.

"You ok? You look like you have the weight of the world on your shoulders," Mark says, leaning against the locker next to mine and eyeing me curiously.

"Just thinking about some school stuff," I say and give him a reassuring smile, grabbing a book out of my locker.

As I close my locker door and turn toward him, he reaches over and gently brushes my hair back away from my face. He looks down at me with a serious expression and says, "If there's anything I can help you with, anything . . . you know I'm here for you."

I can tell by look on his face that he isn't falling for the school excuse. "I know."

Just then I see Sahara walking down the hall looking right at us. I can tell right away that she's not surprised to see us like this. Not surprised, just pissed. She passes so close to us she almost bumps into Mark.

"I talked to Sahara yesterday before I came over to your house. I . . . um . . . told her about us."

"Oh," I say, biting my bottom lip.

"Let's just say she's less than thrilled with me right now."

"Sorry, I don't want to—"

"No. It honestly isn't any big deal." He takes my hand in his own. "Jo, I want you to know, I've never felt this way about anyone before . . . ever."

As I stare into his eyes, my favorite eyes, bit and pieces of the episode last night start to flash in my mind. I push all my doubts away and say, "Me too."

We stand there for a moment just enjoying our little instant of togetherness before heading off to class.

It's lunchtime, and I head over to my usual table. I see Julian already sitting there with that girl Taylor and her friend. I go over and sit down just in time to hear the end of their discussion. Something to do with prom. Is it that time of year already? Our school puts on a Junior and Senior prom every spring with all the typical ostentation. Before now I really never gave it much thought. Honestly I thought it sounded like more trouble than it's worth.

"So Jo, has anyone asked you yet?" Taylor asks, glancing quickly at Julian and then back again to me.

"Uh . . . no," I say, wondering what this girl's interest is in me all of a sudden.

Mark comes over and slips into the seat next to me as she goes on, not taking her eyes off me.

"Well, most of my friends already have dates, now they just need a dress. Crazy, huh? I mean . . . well, if you know who you want to go with, I guess it makes it easier to just go ahead and ask them."

I realize then what this girl's getting at and give Julian a look.

Julian chimes in with a smirk on his face, "That's true. If you know who you want to go with. I mean, if you really like someone, why wait to ask."

Julian's obnoxious behavior isn't lost on Taylor.

Taylor glares at Julian and stands up. "Jerk," she says and storms off with her friend following right behind.

"Why did you do that? You know she's crazy about you."

"Exactly, she is crazy. The girl is a stalker."

I just look at him incredulously and shake my head.

"This seat taken?"

I look up and see Gio staring down at Mark with her usual dripping-with-sexuality voice.

"Uh . . . no," he says and scoots closer to me.

She sits down and, putting her hand on his knee, leans slightly across him to say, "Hi Josephine."

I barely smile as I watch her glance over at Julian, not

taking her hand from Mark's knee.

"I saw both your skits at the talent show," she says, looking from Mark to Julian. "Julian, it's Julian right? You were very . . . audacious. I like that."

"Thanks," he says in an uninterested tone as he takes a bite from his sandwich.

Giving him a quizzical look, she then directs her attention to me.

"So Josephine, has my brother asked you to prom yet?"

Mark straightens up.

"No! I, um—"

"Oh, don't worry, he will. I'm sure most of the girls at this school would just love to go with him, but he's pretty enamored with you," she says matter-of-factly.

Ugh.

I look over at Julian for help, but he's ignoring the whole conversation. Do I tell her about Mark and I? What would I say, I mean . . . are we an actual couple? She eyes me strangely, then decides she's done with the conversation and gets up to leave.

"Oh and Josephine . . . let me know if you need help picking out a dress. You, in a dress that I picked out, on my brother's arm. Let's just say . . . heads would turn." She saunters off without another word.

"Yeah, I better go, too. Class is about to start," Julian says and jumps up, grabs his books, and is gone.

I'm feeling really irritated and confused wondering how things managed to turn out like this in the matter of minutes. Mark starts fumbling around with his books, and I can tell he's stewing. Does he honestly think I have feelings for this guy? I mean, he only gave me a ride home. I let out a big sigh as my frustration starts to get the better of me.

"Mark, I don't know why that girl is determined to set me and her brother up, but honestly I have zero feelings for him and I'm pretty sure he doesn't for me either."

As I sit there searching for some kind of acknowledgement that I'm explaining myself properly, he smiles. A real smile. A smile that sends relief coursing through me, telling me that we're all right.

"Well, I was going to wait until a more . . . appropriate time, but with all the stiff competition. . . "

"Real funny," I say, rolling my eyes.

"No . . . no, really Jo. Will you go to prom with me?"

I'm a little taken aback, and my first thought is how crazy of a lunch this ended up being, but then focusing back on his words, happiness takes hold.

"Mark, there's no one I'd rather go with," I say and wrap my arms around him in a big hug.

As we leave to head to class, I feel something I never thought I ever would about prom. Excited.

12

—

'***ve been putting this off for a few weeks now, so I figure I
better just get it over with. Getting to the dress section,
I just stand there looking at the sea of prom dresses. I'm
wondering now if I should have taken Gio up on her offer,
even if I'm not going with her brother.

Feeling slightly overwhelmed I wander through the
racks feeling the different materials. Most girls would probably look at color or even style but no . . . I'm more interested
in what the dress is made of. Sighing, I finally find a floor-
length champagne-colored one with spaghetti straps. It's
made from some sort of satiny material. Captivated by its
fabric, I rub it next to my face feeling its cool, smooth texture
against my skin.

Realizing that I must look strange, I glance around, but
there isn't anyone here. I purposely came at an off time hoping that I wouldn't run into anyone from school. It's bad
enough I have to do this at all, but to have to try the dresses
on in front of other people. . .

I grab one in my size then start searching for another. I
can't help but feel that prom night is going to be more than
just a stupid school function. I'm not entirely sure what to
expect, but I know what I would like to happen. To take our
relationship to that level would mean everything to me.

I spot a blue dress that looks to be made from a similar
silky material.

As I head in the direction of the dressing room, I remember what Gio said about Sandy wanting to ask me to prom.

I'm still not sure if that is even true. I get the feeling Gio is up to something. I don't trust anything that comes out of her mouth, and I especially don't like the way she always looks at Mark.

I get to the outer door of the dressing room and look around for an attendant. There's no one in sight. As I go through the outer door a bell rings, flooding the area with its obnoxious tune announcing that someone has entered. Looking toward my right I see a long, narrow hall. There are about ten doors on either side met at the end of the hall by a giant full-length mirror. All the doors seem to be ajar, so I must be the only one here. I head toward one of the last doors, closest to the mirror.

As I get to the end of the hallway I hear the doorbell ring again. Ugh, that means someone else will be in here trying something on. I was really hoping to have the place to my-self. I don't look back and dive into the last dressing room. When I walk in I see a small mirror on the wall and a bench off to the side. I hang the dresses on a hook and turn around to shut and lock the door behind me.

When I turn around Sahara is leaning against the door-way, arms folded over her chest, with a smirk on her face.

What is she doing here?

"Shopping for your prom dress?" she says with a glint of anger in her voice. Her beautiful blond hair is pulled back in a ponytail and instead of one of her usual short, color-ful miniskirts, she's wearing tight black pants. Her whole demeanor seems different, almost threatening.

"I just want you to know that I don't need that Neanderthal anymore. I mean, he served his purpose, so throwing him out to the trash . . . well, let's just say, keeping the trash occupied, works well, too."

It takes me a minute to register what she's saying.

"Am I the trash?" I ask feeling very confused and

wondering where this conversation is going.

She stands up narrowing her eyes at me.

"I knew when I got to this school it would be easy to control all these mindless teenagers, especially with the star basketball player at my side. It's been so frigging easy, but you, the special one, you've been a pain in my ass from the beginning. Everybody, always wanting to protect you. . . "

She glares at me.

Moving toward me angrily she says, "The thing is, you really do believe you're just this sweet, sheltered teenage girl with doting parents and best friends that love and support you no matter what. You're so full of shit! Your whole life is full of shit!"

She's standing right in front of me now, and my back is against the wall. What she's saying isn't making any sense.

Cornered like this I can feel my body reacting, starting to have one of my episodes. If she doesn't back off quickly, I'm not sure what will happen.

She looks at me then and I see something in her eyes. Recognition.

"How you feeling, Jo? Feeling a little hot? Maybe your heart's starting to race. Muscles starting to constrict. What, gonna hit me?"

Her face is an inch away from mine. There's hate in her eyes. It's as if she's trying to get me worked up . . . wanting, even knowing how I'm going to react.

I can feel the heat rising within my body. She's right, my muscles are starting to constrict. How does she know about these things that are happening to me?

Feeling trapped, I do the one thing that I'm good at: I open my mouth and say the absolute wrong thing.

"I can see now why leaving you wasn't a problem for Mark. A little less psycho in his life is a good thing."

Before I can even think about what I just said, she grabs

me by the neck and with one arm lifts me up off the ground, pinning me against the wall.

With her hand wrapped around my neck in the strongest grip I've ever felt, I'm barely able to breathe. Instinctively I start to claw at her hand as the pressure becomes overwhelming. I can't believe how strong she is.

With more rage in her voice than I've ever heard, she snarls, "I don't see what makes you so fucking special. You think that stupid brother and sister are going to be able protect you. . . "

I'm beginning to feel lightheaded.

Something changes then and she loosens her grip slightly. She drops me. As I'm bent over, grasping for air, she starts to walk off but then stops in the doorway and turns around.

"Oh I do hope you love birds have a good time, and if I were you, I'd pick the blue one."

Then she's gone, with the dressing room bell announcing her departure a few seconds later.

It takes a few minutes regain my composure. Then I quickly shut and lock the door and just sit on the bench for a while trying to comprehend what's just happened.

At first I think about telling Mark about what's happened. It was assault after all. But then I think that would just worry him, maybe even be enough to make him realize I really am a freak, someone he's better off without.

After pulling myself together, I grab the prom dress I want—the champagne one—and take it to the counter without even trying it on.

"We'll be back soon, Josie," I hear my dad call up to me from downstairs.

"Ok, Dad," I call out. The front door opens and closes and they're gone.

"How long will your dad have to keep working on his grant?" Mark asks, sprawled out on my bed.

I'm flitting around my room getting ready. We are going to a movie tonight, so Mark came by a little early to do one of his new favorite things—watch me get ready.

"He says probably a month or two, but I find with these things it's hard to say."

He's always had to work extra on one thing or another since he's been with the university, but this particular grant has been tough for him. A lot of extra hours, even having to get my mom to help with some of the legwork. They both seem so stressed out lately with it all.

"Yeah, and I'll be glad when he can get some down time again. I haven't gotten to see much of him lately. It would be nice if he were around more."

Mark's lying on his back just staring at the ceiling. I'm sure he's thinking of his own dad and how he'd be happy if he were around to be able to spend any time with him.

Feeling bad I go over to the bed and lean over him. He looks at me and I can see the hurt in his eyes.

"Sorry, I didn't mean to bring up—"

"You didn't. Don't worry." Then he pulls me down for a kiss. He loves to take me off guard with his kisses.

I laugh and try to break free. This just makes him hold onto me more, so I give up and start kissing him back. I love kissing him, the way my entire body starts to come alive.

We continue for a few minutes like that until he sits up abruptly and then pushes me down on the bed so he's above me. He kisses me harder than usual. As the kiss deepens I can feel his need for me grow. He's starting to get desperate.

I want this.

Feeling slightly lightheaded, I kiss him back with all

the same urgency. Our need for each other is becoming overwhelming. I'm so caught up in the moment with him, I don't realize that I'm starting to have a full-blown episode. I can feel the heat generating from deep within. My actions are becoming more intense, more aggressive. I want him . . . all of him.

I yank his shirt up and start fussing with the front of his pants. As I'm attempting to undo his belt, he sits up. I don't care. My mind is racing. Images of the things I want to do with him—do to him—are flashing through my head. I sit up suddenly and push him down.

"Jo, wait. . . "

I hear him, but my need is insatiable. I kiss his stomach. He groans—unable to stop himself—and lightly pushes me away from him.

Panting he says, "Jo, please. I'm having a hard time restraining myself here, but this isn't right. I mean . . . something isn't right. Something isn't right . . . with you."

I'm having a hard time concentrating on what he's saying.

"Jo, your chest!"

The realization of what he could be getting at hits me then.

I look down and all my fears are realized. Light pours forth from my chest. My body feels as though it's on fire. I turn away from him, trying to regain control.

I close my eyes and try to breathe slowly. I feel him put his hand gently on my shoulder.

"Are you all right? Is it something that I did? I didn't mean to. . . "

"No! It's nothing you did," I say turning around to face him, feeling more like myself.

"These strange things that are happening to me . . . they've actually been getting worse lately."

I look away from him as the tears threaten to come. "I

didn't want to tell you I was getting worse. I couldn't tell you . . . couldn't ruin what we have."

"Jo, do you honestly think I wouldn't understand? When I turn and look at him, the look on his face reiterates what he says next. I'm not going anywhere."

He takes me in his arms then and just holds me. I begin to feel all my fears, all my insecurities, melt away.

"Whatever this is that's happening to you, we'll figure it out."

He squeezes me tight and kisses the top of my head as he lets out a big sigh. "I love you, Jo."

Sitting there, him holding me close, I realize for the first time that things really may be all right in the end. Maybe even better than all right . . . maybe perfect.

The next night we try the movie thing again. After what happened last night, Mark and I ended up just staying in my room talking as he held me from time to time.

We figure whatever is wrong with me has to be triggered by hormones. Leaving another message for the old football player is about all we can think to do after an hour of desperate research.

One of the things Mark and I didn't discuss was the glowing light that came from my chest. He actually didn't even ask me about it. It's probably too much to try to even wrap his head around right now. Heck, it's too much for me to wrap my head around.

I hear the doorbell ring downstairs. I can hear Mark and my dad talking. My parents haven't really said much about the fact that we've started seeing each other. I know they've always thought of him as a decent boy. But since they've both been so preoccupied with work lately, I figure they probably haven't given it much thought.

I head down the stairs and smile when I see Mark. Looking as handsome as ever, he watches me come down with that look in his eyes. My heart does its usual flutter.

After saying goodnight to my parents, we head out to his car. He comes around to the passenger side to open the door for me, but before I get in he grabs me in a tight hug.

"I missed you today," he whispers in my ear. He looks at me and leans down to give me a gentle kiss. Smiling at each other we head to the theater. Tonight's already looking up. . .

When we get there I realize how long it's been since I've seen a movie. The place is absolutely packed. As we stand in line for the tickets, I see many familiar faces from school. The same people that hang around each other at school are in their little cliques here, too.

Once we're in our seats, Mark reaches over and grabs my hand. Looking down at our hands intertwined, I think back to the last time I came to a movie. It was with Aiden. I remember at the time wondering what it would be like to be at the movies with Mark. To be sitting next to him instead of Aiden. The thought causes a pang of guilt. I push the thoughts aside, concentrating on the realization that I'm here with him now. Sometimes I still can't believe that so many of my fantasies regarding him have become reality. Being here with him and knowing he's the one person in the world that knows just about everything about me. And he loves me. I smile to myself as the lights go out and the movie starts.

The movie's really good but unable to keep my attention completely. As I sit here trying to keep my mind focused on the plot line, I feel antsy. Needing to shake this fidgety feeling, I excuse myself and head to the bathroom.

In the bathroom I go over to the sink to wash my hands,

hoping the warm water will calm me down a bit. As I look in the mirror I catch sight of my chest. It's beginning to glow ever so slightly. What could be causing me to do this now? Other than feeling a little antsy, I feel relatively normal. I could swear it's getting brighter. Starting to feel panicky I do the one thing that seems to always help . . . get moving. I leave the bathroom and head down a quiet hall toward the back. I see an exit door at the end of it that seems to have been left ajar. I head toward the door thinking that if I could just slip out for a moment and run around, I might be able to ward off this impending episode.

I get to the door and see that there's something underneath it keeping it from closing completely. As I start to squeeze through the narrow opening without disturbing whatever it is that's keeping the door open, I hear a muffled yell from outside. Without thinking, I push the door open and go out.

As I step outside I realize I'm in the back alley behind the theater. Once my eyes adjust to the darkness, I'm able to make out some movement down by a couple of dumpsters that are way off to the right. Some kind of scuffle.

I'm there in a flash.

Gio grunts and doubles over as she's punched in the gut by some guy in black fatigues. Sandy's there then sending the guy flying into the side of a dumpster.

I hear a scream and look over to see another guy dressed just like the first one running toward two blond girls huddled together on the side of the alley.

The shorter girl steps forward as he approaches, and I realize then who she is. It's the blond girl that sang at the talent show, the one who seemed so timid and unsure of herself. Seeing her now, in this situation, she seems anything but unsure.

"Get out of my way, bitch," the guy says and starts to

push her away. Before he has a chance, she reaches out and touches his chest. Just a touch and he's gone. Completely gone. Disappeared.

Sandy's next to her in an instant, panting.

"Where did you send him?"

"Not far enough," the guy says, suddenly coming at Sandy again.

The girl gives Sandy an apologetic look. Swiftly raising his arm, Sandy blocks a punch, but the guy reacts quickly, driving his foot forward into Sandy's abdomen with such force that he's slammed back against the side of the building, banging his head on its bricks. Dazed, he just lies there. I start to run in his direction but then see the guy walk toward the two girls, pulling something out of his jacket.

I look toward Gio, but see she's still fighting off her own attacker.

As the man gets to the girls, the younger one steps forward again. This time he's ready

before she knows what's coming, he strikes her with the back of his hand across the head, sending her to the ground with a thud. The other girl, seeing the smaller one lying on the ground lifeless, stares at the guy approaching and whimpers.

I'm there then, right beside the two of them. The guy sees me, but before I can do or say anything, he pushes the girl down on her back and thrusts some sort of Taser-looking mechanism against her chest. It releases something like an electric charge but quickly gives out. At that exact moment a burst of bright light is expelled from my chest.

Throwing me a scowl, the guy quickly tries again, and this time an electric current shoots from the mechanism and travels directly into the girl's chest. As I stand there stunned at what I'm seeing, the girl starts to convulse violently. Smoke starts to rise up around her. I realize then that the smoke is coming from inside her. I'm frozen as I watch smoke ascend from her mouth and eyes. It's as if I'm watching this poor girl burn alive from the inside out.

The guy stands up, and without even another glance my way, he's gone. The girl lies still, smoke continuing to rise around her. Her eyes are open and staring up into the night sky.

I look over at Gio just in time to see her deliver an elbow strike to the other guy's temple. He crumbles to the ground. Before walking away she stops and watches for a moment as he lies there twitching. Bending down, she grabs his head, and in one fluid motion snaps his neck.

She stands up, adjusting her clothes and hair as if she were about to go out onto a stage, and then walk over to the smaller girl that's now trying to sit up. She says something to her in a low voice as she helps her.

I turn toward Sandy. He's standing up slowly, eyes fixed on me. Walking over he takes my hand and has me sit down beside me.

"You all right, Jo?" he asks weakly.

All I can do is nod as I glance over at that poor girl that only a few minutes ago was scared out of her mind. At least she won't be scared anymore. She won't feel anything anymore.

"We need to get you out of here, but I want you to listen very carefully to what I'm about to tell you."

I nod again.

"Jo, I work for . . . a certain group of people that have been trying to stop these . . . These similar types of killings."

Feeling numb, I wait for him to continue and can tell he's searching for the right words.

"I know that it didn't work out so well tonight, but you have to trust me when I tell you that we've saved lives, many lives. But if we are to continue to save these lives, no one can know about us. Do you understand?"

As his words begin to register, I look over at him and see exactly what I need to see—sincerity.

"So you're telling me I can't tell anyone about this?"

"No one, Jo. To protect those you love, absolutely no one."

I stare into those gray-blue eyes as my mind attempts to wrap itself around all this craziness.

"I understand," I say in almost a whisper.

He sighs, then looks deep into my eyes. It's a reassuring look that instantly makes me feel connected with him.

"I'll call you and we'll plan a time when I can come by your house sometime, ok? I'll explain everything then, I promise."

"Sure."

"Jo, I need you to think about the people you love. You need to get your act together and hurry back. You're on a date, remember?"

How does he know that?

"Don't worry," I say. "The last thing in the world I would ever do is put the people I love in danger."

And with that, I jog back to the door that's still ajar and slip back in. Turning the corner someone grabs me from the side. I look up and it's Mark, and he looks pissed.

"What the hell, Jo?" Right away I want to tell him everything, but don't.

Giving him my most apologetic look, I say, "I'm so sorry. I don't know, it must have been the movie or something, but I started having one of my episodes. It came on so fast. . ."

"I thought it was probably something to do with your . . . anyway, I'm glad you're all right."

"I am," I say wrapping my arms around him.

"I guess I'm not going to be able to let you out of my sight from now on," he says, smiling.

"I like the sound of that," I say and pull him down for a kiss. As my eyes close, the girl's face from the alley flashes in my mind and I gasp.

"What's wrong?"

"Nothing. Forget it."

"C'mon, movie's over. I'm taking you home now."

13

wake up to my cell phone's tune playing in my ear. I slowly reach over and grab it, not recognizing the number I see.

"Hello?"

"Hey Jo, it's Sandy."

When I hear his voice, I sit up as my grogginess immediately dissipates. Images of last night's events flash through my mind.

"I was hoping I could see you sometime today to discuss some things."

"Uh, sure."

"Can I come over in say . . . an hour?"

"Sure."

Then there's another awkward pause.

"Ok, I'll see you soon then."

"Ok."

Then he's gone and I sit there feeling like I must have come across like a mental case. What could I say, though? The things I saw last night left me scared and insecure. I also have this gnawing feeling I'm about to find out something that I probably would rather not know anything about.

And what about Mark? I didn't tell Mark anything about what I saw last night because I was so freaked out, but I can't keep these things from him. If there's one thing I've learned from years of watching TV, it's that keeping secrets is never good for a relationship.

❋

Downstairs in the kitchen there's a big plate of blueberry muffins on the counter with a note under it. I don't even have to read the note to know what it says.

I grab a muffin and wolf it down just in time to hear the doorbell ring.

As I walk toward the door I see Sandy standing there through the glass. Even with the slight distortion of the glass, I'm reminded of how extremely attractive he is. It's almost distracting.

I open the door and am met with those amazing blue-gray eyes. As he steps into the house I see him look around.

"My parents aren't here right now."

He nods and follows me into the living room. It's weird having him in my house. Even though his looks can be intimidating, I find that isn't the reason I'm on edge whenever he's around me. No, it's not his charisma or even the way he looks at me, it's the fact that every time he comes into my life, he causes me problems.

We go into the living room and I straightaway sit down on the couch like a little kid about to get a dreaded lecture. He recognizes my apprehension and sits down right next to me. Looking away he sighs and runs his fingers through his hair, seemingly unsure of how to start. I gaze at the perfect features of his profile, ostensibly so troubled.

"Jo, what I'm about to tell you might seem strange, probably crazy actually, but you have to trust me in that what I tell you is true."

I nod. He sighs.

"There are people that are born with something in their DNA. When these people start experiencing certain hormonal fluctuations or surges in adolescence they . . . change."

"Change, like as in puberty," I ask.

"No, this is different." He stops for a moment. Maybe he's trying to see if my mind can connect the dots quick enough. Seemingly satisfied that I can, he continues.

"There's something in this particular region of the Southwest that's literally acting like a catalyst to this change. It's some kind of energy source."

"What do you mean 'energy source'?"

"We don't exactly know, but we do know that it's what causes the DNA to react the way it does. Causes kids to become different."

"Different?"

"You've been noticing some changes lately, right? The ability to do things other girls your age can't?"

I just stare at him.

"Yeah, I know," he says pausing to give me a look that tells me he understands everything I've been going through.

"Look, you need to know, there's this organization that calls themselves The Order. Their leaders, members of a particular board of directors, also exhibit special . . . attributes. We don't know for sure how long they've been around, but let's just say we have documentation that it's been . . . well, a while."

"What do they have to do with me?"

"Jo, they're the ones responsible for your friend's murder. For all the murders in town."

He stops and looks away for a moment. All I can do is hold my breath as the realization of what he's saying hits home.

"You mean Aiden. . . "

As I say his name, tears sting my eyes. So he went through the same thing that poor girl did last night. Her lifeless face looking up at the sky flashes in my mind.

"The people I work with," Sandy says, "we are trying to protect the others like us."

I look back at him as I realize that he's telling me he's one of these people, like I am, like Aiden was. That we're connected somehow.

I think back on the symptoms I suspected Aiden was having before he died. How similar they were to my own now.

"Everyone that goes through the change shows signs, but we believe there is someone out there who may be exhibiting special abilities above and beyond the typical. Their body is reacting differently. . . "

"How?"

"I'm not exactly sure, but I do know everyone wants to find this person."

"So you're one of these people with special abilities?"

"Yes, I went through my change quite a few years ago."

"What do you mean? You're seventeen."

"Not exactly, one of our abilities is slower than average aging, so we look younger than we are. That's how I'm able to look like a high school student. Able to fit in at your school."

"I wouldn't say you exactly fit in."

Laughing, he says, "I guess you're right. Gio and I probably haven't been as subtle about the whole thing as I'd have wished."

"So Gio's not your sister, I take it?"

"No." He looks at me and smiles at the expression on my face. "I know she may come across a little, well, forward, but if there's one person committed to the cause, it's her. I would trust her with my life."

So Gio's one of these special people too. This group is getting more interesting by the minute. "Why is The . . . Order or whatever killing people?"

"All I know is it has something to do with the energy source. It's a catalyst to the change, but it also feeds our abilities. Something's happening to it. Its power is waning, and if it disappears, so do our abilities. As it is, the supply is becoming more and more limited. Do you remember a large number of serial murders, a while back?"

I nod remembering all about how random the victims had seemed. A couple of them were professional athletes, while one, I remember, was this highly accomplished scientist. I could see how they could possess special abilities. But then some of the people that were killed just seemed pretty normal.

"Around that time is when my organization was formed. A scientist in The Order realized they were killing these people to stop them from using up the energy source. This person, this scientist, couldn't stand back with good conscience and not help these people, so he secretly formed my group. We call ourselves The Circle, and we've been given the task of finding and protecting as many of these people as we can."

My head spins with all the information. It all sounds so crazy, so complicated.

"Jo, you all right?"

"Yeah, I guess it's just a lot to take in," I say, giving him a weak smile.

The doorbell rings then and I jump.

Sandy stands up just as I get a sinking feeling.

"Are you expecting someone," he asks.

"Not really," I say leaving the room to answer it, hoping for the first time in my life it's a solicitor.

Walking to the door, I see that it's Mark. My mind suddenly begins to race as I realize I'm going to have to explain why Sandy's here.

I take a deep breath.

"Hey," I say, giving Mark a welcoming hug. He hugs me back stiffly, which tells me right away that he's not happy with that Porsche sitting in the front of my house. When I draw back from him he gives me a questioning look and then glances into the house, searching.

I take his hand and, bringing him in, shut the door

behind us. As we stand in the foyer I rack my brain trying to think of what to say.

"I was driving by your house on my way home and saw Sandy's car out front. Is everything all right?" he asks.

"Oh yeah, he um . . . just stopped by to talk about. . . " Not knowing what else to say, I just trail off and look down at my feet.

"Jo, what's going on?"

I look up and see Mark looking at me intensely, waiting for me to explain.

I want to protect him from all this, but I know that there's no other way to explain this situation without hurting him in some way.

"Mark, I think Sandy knows something about the weird stuff that's been happening to me lately."

"How? I mean, how does he have any idea what you've been going through. . . ?"

"I don't know, he just does," I say understanding his skepticism.

"Jo, it doesn't make sense. This guy just shows up–"

"Mark, he's had the same symptoms. I know it sounds crazy but he wants to help me get through this, so I can. . . "

It all hits me then. So I can what . . . be normal? I realize as I look at Mark that all I want more than anything is to be normal, but it sounds to me like I'll always be anything but. I'm one of these special people. Special. Yeah right, doesn't sound so special to me—definitely not normal.

I throw my arms around Mark and start to sob as everything that Sandy has told me hits home.

Through my sobs I manage to say, "I'm so sorry."

He pulls away from me and with his eyes concernedly searching mine he says, "Jo, what's going on?"

I take his hand and lead him into the living room. Sandy, standing by the window, turns when he hears us come in. "Jo, are you ok?"

Mark, stepping past me toward Sandy, says, "Obviously not, and I'd like to know what the hell you've been saying to make her so upset."

"I'm trying to help her. Explain things to her that she needs to know for her own . . . safety," Sandy says.

"Her safety? What, you think you're somehow in charge of her safety?"

"Like you're the only one that cares for her, is that it?" Sandy says, raising his voice as he walks towards Mark.

"Guys, please . . . this isn't helping."

Why does everything in my life have to be so complicated? I think, as I stand there looking from one to the other.

I know Sandy just wants to protect me, but Mark's feeling pushed aside right now. I have to tell him what's going on. I mean, it's only fair that he grasp the full scope of what being involved with me entails.

"Sandy, I realize you're just looking out for my best interests, but you can trust Mark. He knows all about what I've been going through. He's helped me so many times."

I look over at Mark. He seems pensive, on-edge.

Sighing, Sandy says, "I get it, Jo. I know what you're going through."

"You do huh," Mark says sarcastically.

Sandy ignores him then starts to leave but not before turning to me to say, "It's just you have to understand that from what I've seen, sometimes the closest person to you is the one person you don't want to get involved."

And with that he walks out.

I look over at Mark, and he's just staring straight ahead. I hate that we have this between us. If I tell him everything, will he be in some kind of danger? Would he even trust that I've told him everything anyway? Ugh.

Then I see it on the window, written across the upper

right hand corner of the glass with some sort of chalk-like substance. Hidden from view unless you were looking directly from this vantage point are the words Don't trust him.

Sandy can't possibly think Mark has something to do with any of this craziness, can he? Mark sits down on the couch, the weight of his emotions so evident as he glances my way. There's no way Mark would ever—could ever—do anything to hurt me, or anyone else for that matter. Sandy's just being excessively cautious or slightly paranoid. Either way, I trust Mark completely.

I walk over to him and climb on his lap, straddling him as he stares down at me seemingly relieved. I take his face in my hands and look into his eyes.

"No matter what's going on in my life, I want you to know, that I love you."

end up telling Mark all of what Sandy had told me. He listens intently all the while and tells me all the things that I hope to hear. All the things I need to hear. That's when my cell phone rings.

"Yeah, someone left this number on my machine. Wanted to talk about my, uh . . . football days."

It's Tom Perlow, the guy Mark and I had been trying to get a hold of. The guy we were hoping could explain what was happening to me. That was before Sandy did.

"Yes, my name's Josephine. I was hoping I could talk to you about—"

"Listen, I know why you're calling. I wasn't going to call you back, don't need any aggravation in my life, but things have changed. There's some things you need to know."

"Some things I need to know?"

"I need you to meet me somewhere."

Meet him somewhere? Why? "Can't we just talk now?"

"No. Listen, I don't want you freaking out on me but that phone you're on, your house . . . well, it ain't exactly secure. At least as far as I'm concerned."

Oh boy, he's one of these conspiracy freaks. Great. "Where do you want to meet?"

"Meet me at the old Bueller High School in, say, half an hour."

"The old one, you mean the one that's closed down?"

"You got it. Park around back and I'll be in the boys' locker room. Oh, and bring your boyfriend . . . I want to meet him too." He hangs up.

✳

We pull up to the old abandoned school and drive around back. The grass is overgrown all around old, rundown athletic equipment lying sporadically over the grounds. An old white pickup trucked parked by the building tells me he must already be here waiting.

"I don't like this," Mark says grabbing my arm before I can enter the building.

"I know it's weird, but I think he's just being . . . uh, ultra cautious."

"You sure we shouldn't talk to Sandy about this guy first? I mean, he—"

"No. It just seemed like he had something he really needed to tell me. Like he had some information that would help me or something."

"But why would he want to meet me," Mark asks.

"I don't know. You know, maybe you shouldn't go in."

"Yeah right, I'm gonna let you go in there by yourself. Come on, let's go," he says and walks in.

Walking down a short, narrow hallway, we get to a door labeled boys' locker room. Mark walks in first and grabs my hand to keep me slightly behind him. When we enter we see him leaning against the wall right in front of us. I was expecting to see a man in his sixties, but he couldn't be more than thirty. Outdoorsy type with tan, familiarly flawless skin and blond hair. Attractive in a lumberjack type of way.

"So you guys came after all," he says straightening up and checking me over with more scrutiny than I like.

"Yes, uh . . . hi Mr. Perlow," Mark says extending his hand toward him.

Ignoring the gesture, he starts talking hurriedly. "Look, it's nice to meet you and all that crap, but you gotta know a few things before I blow outta here. First off giant, you should watch your back too. She ain't completely changed yet, and to be honest, since she's so friggin . . . uh, let's say different to be nice."

Mark chimes in angrily, "Hey buddy, watch yourself. You have something to say then—"

"Ok, ok . . . sorry. Just not used to interacting with people much anymore."

"Why?" I ask stepping forward.

He immediately steps back away from me, then catches himself and gives me a weak smile.

"I'm sure you read all about my football glory days in those ancient papers. Good catch by the way. I forgot about that obscure paper and that stupid article. Thought I covered all my tracks."

"Yeah, well we were looking for someone with similar symptoms to my own."

"Similar to you. Maybe a little, but you, you're—" he looks at Mark then continues. "Anyway, I went through my change a while back. Man, before that I could barely throw the ball straight, and my speed, well it just sucked. Then I started feeling different off and on . . . changing. Puberty, my ass. All of a sudden I'm the best player on the team, the star. Sure it helped me with the chicks and all, so you'd think I'd be cool with it, but no . . . I just felt like a freak."

I'm suddenly feeling like we have more in common than he realizes.

"And you know what was worse, the fact that nobody said shit about it. Hell, maybe they were afraid too. I don't know, maybe I'm crazy . . . was crazy, but I just couldn't accept it. So I took off. Jumped in my car and started driving. Got a few states away before I started feeling it. Feeling like shit, like I was dying or something. The new kickass feeling I'd gotten used to was fading. Maybe I was just feeling normal again, I don't know. All I know is I couldn't hack it, so I headed back. Wasn't long into the trip back that I started feeling the effects again. Crazy, huh? I mean, this power source thing."

I start thinking about this connection we all have to this power source. Was I going to be so dependent on it too?

He sighs before continuing, "Now this is the shit you gotta hear. When I got back I was approached by these five people. Five people that had just recently gone through the change. They wanted to talk to me, find crap out about me. I didn't like the looks of them. Now that girl, she was hot, but I don't know, she gave me the creeps."

He looks at Mark, "You know man, hot enough to bang, but made my skin crawl. That was my instinct kicking in gear. Been using it ever since, like with you two. Wanted you here, in front of me. To get a feel for you. Needed to figure out myself if you were gonna be the kind of people that would be on the good side or well . . . evil side. You see, it's black and white really. You either do what's right, or you don't."

"Are you talking about The Order? Are they the . . . evil side?" I ask incredulously.

"Smirk all you want, but yeah, that's what I'm talking about. That organization was started by the same five people that came to me that day. They're messed up in a lot of evil shit. Stuff that'd keep you up at night, if you know what I mean."

"What kinds of stuff?"

"You'll find out soon enough. Things ain't what they seem for you . . . hell, for either of you."

"What isn't as it seems?" I ask more for Mark's sake then my own.

"All I'm saying is, you gotta make a choice. Things are gonna get pretty fucked up for you, but you still gotta choose. It sucks, I know, believe me I know."

"So, your telling us not to join the organization. But I'd never—"

"Yeah, you say that now, but, they gotta way of—just ask Sandy. By the way, you can trust him."

I glance up at Mark but can't read him.

"Anyway I gotta go," Tom says and heads to the door leaving me wondering what exactly he had even told us.

"Josephine, I do hope to see you again, because then, you'll be asking the right questions."

Then he's gone.

The whole way home Mark and I run through every thing he said, trying to fill in the blanks and read between the lines. For some weirdo woods guy, I get the impression there's more to him than I realize. Just when I thought things couldn't get more complicated.

I just can't shake this feeling of dread today. Ever since I woke up it feels as though there's a dark cloud hovering over me. I really don't want to go to school and hear about this weekend's most recent murder. Horrible images come to me then. That poor girl, just lying on the ground, burned.

Even though I don't feel hungry I run down to grab a quick bowl of cereal. After wolfing it down and saying good-bye to my parents, I race out the door just in time to see Mark pull up.

Once I'm at school I realize no one is really talking about the murder much at all. All anyone seems to be thinking about is the upcoming prom. The organizing committee, headed up by the super outgoing and totally obnoxious

Samantha Winters, is in full swing with all the planning and relentless promoting. Don't get me wrong, I'm actually looking forward to going, but I wouldn't say I'm giddy about it.

While searching for a book in the usual mess that is my locker, Sandy comes up to me. "Here, let me help you with that," he says, taking the book I need out of the bottom of the large heavy pile.

"Thanks," I say giving him a slight smile, lingering longer than I should on that handsome face.

He then leans toward me and whispers, "Jo, I know I laid a lot on you yesterday and I'm sorry for leaving so abruptly. I shouldn't have left you in that situation. I apologize for that."

"Sandy . . . about what you wrote on the window. You can't honestly believe that Mark is involved in any of this?"

"Jo, I know this is hard for you. All of this is hard . . . but I have reason to believe that he is somehow connected to one of the scientists working for The Order. I'm just not sure how."

"You must be wrong. I mean, I trust Mark wholeheartedly. Completely," I whisper.

"Jo, just watch your back. Please. There's more at stake here than just your heart." And with that, he walks away.

When the last bell rings, I pile out of the classroom with the other students feeling as though we're finally escaping fifty minutes of a prison sentence.

As I walk down the hall toward my locker I notice Sahara standing there watching me. Honestly, since our little altercation I haven't really seen her, but now I get the feeling she isn't completely over her issues with me. Ignoring her, I get to my locker and grabbing the books I'll need for the night, just linger for awhile.

Out of the corner of my eye I see Sahara slam her locker and walk off briskly. I think back to what happened in the dressing room . . . what she was capable of. And what she did to Julian in the parking lot. I begin to wonder, could she be like me and Sandy? The thought sends chills up my spine. I think then about her connection with Mark. All of a sudden I'm not feeling so good.

Who do I believe . . . trust?

The hall has almost cleared out completely. Mark walks up. "Everything all right?"

"Of course," I say and go up on my tippy toes to give him a kiss.

He smiles and says, "I hope there's more where that came from. You want to get together and study?"

"You better believe it." I say, grabbing his hand to leave.

As we walk outside to his car, I notice Sandy's Porsche is still parked out front. I wonder what he's still doing here. Most students have gone home by now as the parking lot is pretty empty.

I glance up at Mark and can tell he's noticed Sandy's car also. I squeeze his hand and when he looks down at me I give him my best loving smile. My need to reassure him probably comes from my guilt over being such a weirdo freak in the first place. If I wasn't one of these "special people," Mark and I wouldn't have issues.

Once I'm in Mark's car, I suddenly realize I've forgotten a book I need for an assignment that's due tomorrow.

"I was hoping to spend less time actually doing home-work," Mark says, his eyes smiling at me.

"Although you have no idea how tempting that is, I really have to get this done tonight," I say, leaning over and kissing him.

"Well, we better go get that book," he whispers and then

begins to kiss me more urgently.

I finally push away, laughing. We walk back toward the school hand in hand.

As we're crossing the parking lot, movement draws my attention to the edge of the building. As we walk closer, I realize it's Julian and Sahara, and they seem to be in another heated argument. My pulse starts to quicken as I think back to the last time these two argued. Mark seems to understand and follows as I head toward them.

All my senses are telling me that my friend might be in some sort of danger. I see Julian abruptly turn around and head into a nearby door with Sahara following right behind. When they both disappear into the building, I run toward the same door they just went through. Mark is right behind me.

As I'm standing in the middle of hallway trying to figure out which way they went, Gio bursts through the doors right behind us. When I spin around and see her—she's panting and gives me an exasperated look.

I hear a loud thud down a smaller hall to the right and immediately take off in that direction. When I get to where the hall starts, I stop. It's a long, narrow hall with about eight doors on either side. I wait and listen, hoping that another noise will give me an indication of which classroom they have gone into. Mark and Gio seem to be trying to anticipate my next move, or maybe they just think I'm crazy. Either way, I don't have time to dwell on it as another strange thudding noise causes me to take off running. I notice it then . . . an open door on the left at the end of the hall. Before I can reach it, Gio has passed me and is headed in.

Just as I get to the door, Mark swings me around. He pushes me back so he can go into the room first. He stops when he gets to the doorway so I have to maneuver around him to see what's going on.

This room is our high school's old shop class. It isn't used anymore, but all the tools and old cutting saws are still cluttering up its four large wooden tables.

That's when I see him. Julian lying unmoving on his back with Sahara standing over him looking toward Gio. She quickly grabs a round metal saw blade off of a table beside her and slings it at Gio, striking her in the head. As her head is thrust to the side from the impact, she falls down. Stunned, she looks up as blood begins to run down the side of her face from the large gash above her eye.

At that moment Sahara turns her attention back to Julian and quickly produces a large screwdriver. I yell out her name. Surprised, she pauses and glares at me, but is still able to thrust the screwdriver into Julian's body.

I leap toward him. I have to get to him. But Gio is there first, knocking Sahara over the table with a flying side kick. She reaches down and pulls the screwdriver out of Julian as I stare in horror. Giving me a strange look, he just lies there unmoving. Gio pushes me out of the way suddenly as Sahara thrusts the table to the side with such a force it smashes to pieces against the wall. Damn, that girl is so unnaturally strong.

In a flash, Sahara's right in front of Gio with a hand strike to her chest. Gio quickly recovers and comes at Sahara with a knife. Where did she get that? Gripping the handle of the knife so the blade is coming out of the bottom of her hand, she tries to slice it across Sahara's throat but misses when she pulls her head back just in time.

Sahara, pushed up against another one of the large wooden tables, slams her foot down on Gio's knee, causing it to buckle underneath her. As Gio attempts to regain her balance, Sahara quickly kicks her in the stomach. Gio, bent over and gasping for breath, sees Sahara reach for another sharp-looking metal tool that's lying to the side. Before Sahara gets a chance to use it, Gio takes the knife and slashes her forearm. As the blade slices through flesh and muscle, Sahara cries out, pulling her arm back and stumbling backward.

Mark, seeing that Gio is still seemingly unable to completely catch her breath and struggling to stand, comes over to help her. As he does, Sahara kicks him from behind, sending him sprawling to the floor face first.

With one arm dangling by her side, she uses her other to grab Gio by the hair and smash her face down against the hard wood table. I hear a terrible cracking noise and see blood splatter across the floor as she throws Gio aside. The thrust causes the knife to fly out of Gio's hand and land on the floor by Sahara. Sahara smirks then swiftly scoops it up, positioning herself above Gio. "You can't protect her, bitch!"

Mark is up and pushes me to the side, putting himself between us. Looking at me, he yells, "Jo, get the hell out of here!"

I can't leave him with this crazy person. Not after seeing what she's capable of, not after what she's done to Julian and Gio. I just stand there looking at him as he yells again for me to leave.

She laughs then. A laugh that sends chills down my spine.

"Cut the act, Mark. You can try to save your little girlfriend, but I'm going to kill her . . . gut her actually. Yes . . . I've given it some thought."

Mark stands his ground and yells again for me to leave. Sahara's eyes narrow and she spins toward Mark, kicking him in the face and sending him flying back.

Sandy runs through the door and stops, seemingly in a state of shock.

Sahara sees Sandy and, realizing that her advantage is about to change, lunges at Mark with the knife, but before she is even able to barely move . . . I react.

One quick burst. That's all it takes.

When it's over, I look over at Sandy and he's frozen in place, staring at me in disbelief. Mark's look is different. He seems horrified, maybe even afraid. Afraid of what . . . of me?

Then I see her. Sahara is laying flat on her back on the floor, her eyes open, staring straight ahead. Where her chest and stomach once were is a huge hole. All around her lay bloody chunks . . . bits and pieces of what is now missing from the middle of her body.

I stare at her lifeless face and try to comprehend what just happened, what I just did to her. I look back at my hand and see nothing . . . not a scratch. I keep searching my hand for something, anything. Some indication that what just took place could possibly have truly happened.

I'm brought back from my thoughts as I look over and see Sandy helping Gio up. Not taking her eyes off me, she says to him, "She's the one. She has to be the one."

Sandy goes over to Julian. Although there's quite a bit of blood on his shirt, I realize the wound must not be too extreme. Sandy helps him up, but neither one of them can seem to take their eyes off of me.

I start to walk over to Mark, but he cringes back ever so slightly. He's scared of me. He saw what I did and he's scared, of me—the freak.

As I feel the sobs coming, I turn and run. Run away from any chance of having that life I so desperately wanted. A life with the only person in the world I could ever love.

15

keep running until someone finally grabs me from behind. I turn around and there's Sandy. He catches me as I collapse in his arms sobbing. As he holds me, stroking my hair, I begin to feel calmer. We just sit there like that for a while. I look around and realize I must have run out to the track. We're in the grassy area on the far side of the track away from the school. I can see that no one is around.

"I'm so sorry," he says, his breath raspy with emotion. "If I had known it was you. . . "

"What's wrong with me?"

He just stares at me. I can tell he's trying to figure out exactly what he's going to say to me. Contemplating the right words to choose.

"There's nothing wrong with you. You're just . . . different from the rest of us. Jo, you're the one everybody's been looking for. I thought . . . I mean, I could have sworn it was this other girl, Ava, but it's you. You're the one who will change things."

I put my head back against his chest as I try and decipher his words. As he strokes my hair and whispers to me that I have nothing to worry about, I start to believe him and begin to let my body and mind slip into a quiet, peaceful place. He just holds me as I give into this feeling and fall asleep.

He shifts his weight, and I jolt awake. How long have I been here with him? How could I fall asleep at a time like this? He smiles down at me and asks, "How are you feeling?"

Ignoring his question I break away from his hold on me.

"How long was I asleep?"

"Not long," he says and starts to help me up. "I'm glad you rested. You seem to be more like yourself now, which . . . will make it easier."

"Make what easier?"

"Jo, you have to come with me. I have to keep you safe."

"What? I can't go anywhere. I have to go home. Have to find Julian and see if he's all right. I have to talk to . . . Mark."

Sandy brushes my hair away from my face as I look up at him. I can tell he really does seem bothered that I'm upset.

"Jo, you have to believe me when I say, I understand what you're going through. Trust me, I do. But . . . if you love these people, you'll get as far away from them as possible."

"I can't just leave them . . . how could I. . . "

"Jo, you're not just leaving them. You're saving their lives. No one, and I mean no one, is as important to The Order as you are. They will do anything to get you."

"But I have to know if everyone's all right," I practically yell at him.

"I know, and you will, I promise, just as soon as I get you somewhere safe."

"I'm not going anywhere with you unless I go home first. I need some things and I need to see my parents. I have to see them."

"If that's what it takes to get you to come with me . . . to protect you, then ok, but we need to make it quick. Every minute we're there, well . . . let's just make it quick," he says and gives me a weak smile before grabbing my hand and pulling me along with him.

By the time we get to his car, we're practically running. He uses his remote to unlock the door and then helps me in the passenger side. He runs around to the driver's side and hops in.

Within seconds we are off and racing in the direction of my house. At least I hope that's where we're going. Leaning over me, he opens the glove box. He grabs a phone out and starts dialing.

"Hey." I hear him say into the phone.

Everything goes by in a blur.

"We're going to her house for a moment." Then there's a pause before he continues, "I know. It's unavoidable. After that, my place . . . call you later." Then he hangs up and leans back over to put the phone back in the glove box. When he closes the door to the box, it makes a clicking sound, which I figure must be some sort of locking mechanism.

He's driving extremely fast.

"Everything ok?" I ask, raising my eyebrows quizzically.

He looks over and seeing the look on my face, smiles. It's a sweet smile, and I'm reminded how amazingly good-looking he really is.

"Just thinking about how exactly I'm supposed to keep you safe when I can't seem to say no to any of your demands," he says and then laughs to himself.

"Who was that on the phone?" I ask.

"Gio."

"And?" I ask

"She has Julian and Mark with her right now. She's called people from our group and they are taking care of the . . . body," he says glancing at me concernedly.

I'm reminded that I killed a girl. I mean, granted she probably would have killed us all if she had the chance, but still . . .

Sandy reaches over and grabs my hand. My first instinct is to pull away, but I don't want to hurt his feelings, so I just sit there and let him hold it for a moment before he lets go.

"Jo, there's a few things we need to discuss before I can

let you go into your house."

"Ok," I say, dreading what he might say at this point.

"I think it's safe to assume that not only was Sahara one of our kind, but she must have been with The Order. I have no idea, though, why she was after Julian, and why she hadn't tried to kill you before."

I think then about the dressing room. She obviously knew something, but even though she could have taken me—or worse—at that moment, she didn't. I remember the fight with Julian in the parking lot and his reaction to the whole thing.

"I think Julian might be involved. He's my friend, I know that, so it must be that he found something out and was trying to protect me."

"Maybe Jo, but we need to be careful. Not everybody is looking out for you"

I look over at him and realize that he means every word he's saying. I truly believe he would stop at nothing to protect me.

"Now, when you get in there, it's imperative that you act as though nothing is wrong. You have to figure out a way to get back out of the house without causing suspicion."

"I'm just going to leave them? Leave my parents?" I say, starting to feel the sobs threatening to return.

He pulls to the front of my house and puts the car in park.

"Jo, I know. But remember, if you don't, they could get hurt, or worse. Do you understand what I'm saying?"

"I just think I should tell them something. Explain the situation somewhat."

"You don't want them to know anything about your leaving. Please, trust me when I tell you that hurting them now could save lives later."

I remember what Tom said and decide to trust him. He hasn't given me a reason not to. "Ok."

He gives me a faint smile before I jump out of the car and head to the front door. I pause for a moment, gathering my strength and sorting through my thoughts before I start to go in.

The door is unlocked. That's strange, I think. I push the door open and walk in.

"I'm home," I yell. "Sorry I'm late . . . had a last-minute meeting at school," I say as I walk through the house. Both my parents' cars were in the driveway.

After checking the office, I run up to their room, thinking that maybe they're getting ready to go out or something.

In their room, everything's exactly the way it usually is . . . perfectly neat and orderly.

I run back downstairs to the kitchen. They would have left a note for me if they'd gone out. I stand there racking my brain, trying to remember if they had mentioned anything. I love my family, don't get me wrong, but in this situation I wish we weren't so out of touch with each others' lives.

Unsure of what to do next, I head up to my room to get a few things.

I can feel the tears start to sting my eyes at the thought that I'm going to have to leave them. I get the sinking feeling things will never be the same. How could they be?

I walk in my room and stop in my tracks as I see it hanging there. My prom dress. I had hung it over my closet door so it wouldn't get wrinkled, and it hits me that this is exactly where it's going to stay. Walking over to the dress I rub its smooth, soft fabric over my face to dry my tears. I look down and see that I smudged it with the remnants of whatever makeup happened to be left on my face.

I go over to my closet and grab a bag. I start stuffing it

with whatever clothes I can. I head to the bathroom to grab a few essentials. I realize my parents are going to speculate that I must have run off, especially if I took the time to pack. Recognizing this gives me a sense of relief. They won't understand why I left, but at least they will know I did it of my own accord and wasn't taken or anything.

I walk back in my room with my hands full and head over to the bag sitting on my bed. It was really only a second. A split second where something just didn't seem right. Where something caught my eye and instantly my senses sharpened and my heart rate quickened.

I can feel my muscles begin to contract involuntarily. I instinctively find myself regulating my breathing, trying to stay calm. As I sift through the bag seemingly organizing its components, I swiftly glance at the one thing that has now registered as a sign that things aren't right. My keyboard is sitting in its usual spot in front of my computer on my desk, but smeared across five of the keys is something red. Something red that wasn't there this morning. Blood.

Somewhere in the back of my head I'm scared and want to take off for the door. But this other, new evolving side of me, is quickly sizing up the situation and has already noticed three other blood smudges around my room and have heard a slight creaking of a door downstairs.

How am I able to hear that? Another part of my metamorphosis?

As I slowly zip the bag up I notice a faint hint of that glow coming from my chest. I take a deep breath but it doesn't seem to help my impending episode. I think about Sahara and am suddenly feeling sorry for the poor soul that may be waiting to cause me harm.

I swing the bag over my shoulder, unconsciously grab a pen off my desk, and head for the stairs. When I get to the top of the stairs, I pause. With my senses heightened, my body reacts knowing full well the scope of the situation.

Instead of using the stairs, I push off the railing and leap to the floor below. His movements are fast, but not fast enough. A man dressed exactly like those two men behind the movie theater grabs my arm. Before I'm able to even think about what I'm doing, the pen I had been holding in my hand has been thrust into his temple. As he falls to the ground, the next man is already on me. He slams me against the wall, wrapping his hands around my throat and lifting me off the ground. I'm instantly reminded of Sahara and this famous move she used on me not that long ago.

As I gasp for air, trying to pull his fingers from my throat, I look over in disbelief and see the first man has pulled the pen out of the side of his head and seems to be coming to his senses rather quickly. How could he. . .

Sandy busts through the door and with amazing speed runs right up to the man that has me in his iron clasp. He loses his grip on me as Sandy swings him around, shoving that familiar mechanism right into his chest. It falters, and the man punches him in the gut. Sandy grunts and falls forward onto his knees. As he raises his fist to deliver a punch to Sandy's head, I shove him, causing him to lose his balance and fall to the side.

The first man, eyes locked on Sandy, lunges at him with a knife. That same odd type of knife Gio had earlier. Sandy swings around, obviously not as incapacitated as he seemed, and in one swift motion grabs the hand clutching the knife and thrusts it into the guys side, just missing his chest. The man snickers as he begins to slowly pull the blade from his body.

The other man has me now. His arm is around my neck, choking me in such a grip that I'm starting to feel weak and lightheaded. Sandy tries to come around to help me, but the first man is there with a punch to his jaw. It sends his head to the side momentarily, but he turns back around quickly and blocks the man's next punch before delivering a knuckle strike to the same temple that I'd stabbed earlier. The man screams out in pain, and I see Sandy head toward him again before everything gets blurry and I black out.

16

Everything looks hazy as I try to open my eyes. Blinking, I try to focus until I'm able to see what looks like someone gazing down at me. I can see her now, her blond hair framing an angelic face.

"Hi Josephine," she says, grinning at me.

"Hi," I say groggily as I sit up. Glancing around I realize I'm sitting on a large brown leather couch. I seem to be in some sort of modern-looking log cabin with extremely high ceilings and a pitched roof. Directly in front of me is a tremendous stone fireplace with an open hearth. Although I get the feeling this space is intended to feel rustic, it's anything but.

On either side of the couch is a chair that seems to be upholstered from the hide of some exotic animal. Whatever the material is, it's nothing like I've ever seen. Hanging above the room is an enormous chandelier made of rod iron. Although its size is quite spectacular, the light that it casts throughout the room is soft and subtle.

My eyes are drawn to the fireplace. Perfectly centered above the hearth is a prominently placed large metal circle. Etched within the metal are strange symbols.

"How are you feeling?" the girl asks. I realize then who she is, the girl from the talent show . . . the one that was also in the alley behind the movie theater.

"Uh, fine but . . . where am I?"

"I'm Ava," she says, ignoring my question. "He's been so worried about you. You know . . . you and I are the only people he's ever brought here."

"Where's Sandy?"

"He'll be back. Had to go see the others about something," she says, looking up at me pleasantly.

"What others?" I ask, getting a better look at this place. Off to the side of the large room is a kitchen. The cabinetry is a fancy-looking dark wood with inlaid tiles. The appliances look to be about as modern as they come, and over to the left is a large table made of the same fancy wood as the kitchen cabinets. The entire place is accented with rod iron matching the chandelier.

"You know, I'm not surprised that you're the one they're all looking for. I mean, it makes more sense," she says, watching me.

I'm beginning to realize that talking to this girl is like talking to a brain-teaser. "Ava, right? Listen, I really have no idea what's going on here. Where's Sandy?"

"He loves you, you know."

I'm really starting to think that this girl is batty.

"Who did he go talk to?"

"People like us. Well, not exactly like us," she says and walks over to the kitchen, leaving me more confused than before. She really has a knack for clearing things up.

"So it's that group that Sandy belongs to? The Circle or whatever, the one that's helping to protect me?" I ask.

Over to the side of the kitchen is a spiral staircase that seemingly leads to a large loft area above. I have to say, with all its nooks and crannies, this has got to be the most interesting place I've ever been in.

"Yep, and now that they found you, well, I guess we're all saved," she says, following right behind me.

I swing around to face her then, wondering what the heck she's talking about. "What do you mean we're all saved? Because of me?" I ask, giving her a confused look.

She just smiles at me and then, moving her attention to my chest, reaches out to touch it. As I stare at her, wondering what the heck she's doing, I close my eyes instinctively as my body suddenly feels as though it's free falling. It only lasts a couple of seconds, but it's just long enough to make my stomach roil in response.

Ava and the room are gone now and I find myself standing in the middle of a strange bedroom. How the hell did I get in here? That girl, Ava, must have done something to send me here. Like she did to that guy behind the movie theater.

I see a bathroom over to the side and head in that direction. My stomach has settled down but I'm slightly lightheaded. I walk in the bathroom and it has the same eclectically masculine feel about it. These walls are marbled, which causes the lighting to bounce off of everything in a way that it looks shiny and sleek.

I head over to a large pedestal sink and turn on the water. The water begins to flow out of a long slit in the wall as if it were a waterfall. Staring at the water as it flows from the wall, I can't help but begin to feel a bit overwhelmed.

Things have been moving so fast it's almost as if I'm numb to it all. I feel as though my entire life has been turned upside down. I start to think then about my parents and Mark. My heart rate increases, so I quickly push these thoughts from my head. I can't go there right now.

I turn the water off and walk quickly through the bedroom to a door on the other side. Exiting the bedroom I see that I'm still in the cabin but have ended up upstairs somehow. I see the top of the spiral staircase and head down. It takes me around in four complete circles before I'm at the bottom. There's Ava, smiling at me with the same sweet but clueless look on her face.

"I thought you might want to lie down or freshen up a bit."

"So you . . . sent me up there? How did you. . . "

"It's just something I've been able to do ever since I started changing. If I can control it, I've found it to be quite useful."

"What if you can't control it?" I ask. But I'm not sure I want to know.

Still looking at the floor and using the edge of her foot to trace the tile in an anxious manner she says, "If I can't control it, well people . . . just disappear."

Disappear . . . disappear, where?

She looks up at me and I see pain. The pain in her eyes that tells me something bad has happened to this poor girl.

Then she hugs me saying, "I'm glad you're special like me."

Special like her. I've never thought of myself as special. A freak maybe, but not special. As I hug her back, I do feel a certain kinship toward her. Special or not, she and I seem to be connected in some way. Bonded together by the fact that we are…what? Different. Special.

"I never got a chance to really thank you," Ava says.

"Thank me for what?"

"For helping me with my song at the talent show. When I heard about the show, I really wanted to sing. I guess I didn't realize how scary it would be until I was up there staring out at all those faces. It was like my mind just went blank. I've never really been able to do much when I'm under pressure."

"Well, I think what you did was really brave. And you sang beautifully."

"Thanks."

"I didn't even know you went to my school."

"I don't."

"Then how did you. . . "

"When Sandy told me about the show, I really wanted to sing, so he figured no one would notice that I wasn't a student. I think maybe he talked with someone or something, I don't know. Sandy's always doing sweet things like that."

I think about Sandy and how's he helping me now.

"He's been watching over me ever since. . . " she says, then looks away as tears come to her eyes. I can tell the memory is painful for her as she stares out in silence, her blond hair falling over her small shoulders. She seems so defeated, so sad, but I'm at a loss for what to say to comfort her, so I just sit here hoping my presence is enough.

"She would get angry sometimes. Probably because my dad wasn't there anymore, I don't know." Looking at me then in the most sincere way, she says, "I loved her . . . I love my little sister. Just wanted to protect her, that's all."

"You have a little sister?"

Tears start rolling down her cheeks as she continues, "I didn't want her to start hurting Sadie the way she hurt me, just wanted to protect her. All I wanted to do was protect her."

"Your mom would hurt you?" I ask. She flinches when I say the word "mom."

"She was always quiet afterward . . . never sorry, just quiet."

When she looks back at me then, there's a different look in her eyes. Not the sad girl from a moment ago. Now there's a sharpness to her. A quick spark of anger that flashes, making me pause. Makes me practically hold my breath as I wait for what she has to say next.

"That's fine, she can hurt me . . . but she won't hurt Sadie. I won't let her."

Then the spark, the memory, is gone and Ava blinks

before changing her whole demeanor. I just sit there hanging, waiting for the story to continue, but I can tell her train of thought has switched again.

"Whatever happened . . . I'm so sorry."

She smiles but doesn't say a word.

Ava jumps up when she hears the door open and runs over to Sandy, giving him a big hug. I'm surprised at how relieved and happy I am to see that handsome body walk in, void of any injuries, just smiling. Instantly my mind erupts with questions.

"Hey Jo," he says, laughing as Ava hangs from him. I can tell from her reaction she's crazy about him.

"So what have you girls been up to?"

"Just filling her in on everything," she says, looking at me now with a big grin. All I can do is give her a weak smile and shrug my shoulders.

"Oh good, then she's all up to speed," he says winking at me.

Sandy has brought dinner for us, and when I smell it my stomach growls. While we eat, I don't say much as I watch Sandy and Ava interact. Whatever happened seems to have bonded them together as close as any brother and sister I've ever known.

Once we're done eating, Ava goes on to tell her story about the first time she saw me. How she was paralyzed with fear standing on that stage until I caught her eye. How she'll never forget how I was there for her to save her from total embarrassment. It's when she starts pointing out my physical attributes to him that I find myself blushing uncontrollably.

When she's done, she gives us each a quick look and says she's tired and heads upstairs to bed. Great. Talk about leaving me feeling totally awkward.

"Uh, sorry about that," he says eyeing me oddly. "I guess

she has it in her head that you and I are . . . well, maybe she thinks she's helping us out. You know, payback for being there for her."

"What happened?" I ask.

Sandy lets out a sigh and glances toward the stairs before saying, "I don't know if anything has ever been easy for her. Her dad left her mom when she and her sister were both very young. Not long after that, I guess, her mom started hitting her. Ava says she remembers a time before it all began but I don't know . . . maybe it's her way of hoping that their was ever any good in her mother. Whatever the case, she's had it rough."

The thought of anyone hitting that sweet girl sickens me.

"From what I gather, until the incident, her mother had always just taken her anger and frustration out on her, never her sister. But something must have changed that day, I don't know. She's never talked about exactly what happened . . . what made her snap. All I know is she felt like she needed to protect her sister, so she used her ability."

He looks at me then with an expression I can't read. "But she was able to protect her sister. Her mom somehow wound up in the middle of a busy road that ran right in front of their house. Eyewitnesses and the driver of the bus that hit her say it was as if she appeared out of thin air. One minute everything's normal, and the next this woman is standing in the middle of the road. The bus never even had time to slow down.

"Oh my God. . . ," I say, envisioning the scene it must have been when she was hit.

"I'm not saying she didn't deserve it, but killing your mom has got to mess you up a bit. In her case, it has. . ."

Sandy stands up and walks over by the fireplace. Flipping

a switch, fire erupts from underneath the logs and they start burning. The entire ambiance of the room changes instantly, and I stare in amazement at the switch that made it all possible. I walk over and sit down on the soft brown leather couch.

I watch Sandy stand in front of the fireplace staring into the flames. The soft glow of light reflecting off his perfectly bronzed features. He stands there with his arms crossed seemingly deep in thought. I wonder how many times he's probably stood here, the same look on his face, same set to his shoulders. For a moment I feel sad for him, for this life that is so complicated and deadly.

"How did you end up being the one that gets to take care of . . . the special one?"

He looks over at me and seems a little shocked.

He comes over and sits next to me on the couch. "Almost everyone I know like us, well . . . let's just say we all have our stories. Mine is similar, just slightly different circumstances is all."

Looking away from me then, and I see a pain that's apparent.

I can't bear to watch him like this a second longer, so I do the only thing I can think of. I slide closer to him and wrap my arms around his neck. I want him to know how very sorry I am for all that's happened to him in the past.

He seems slightly taken aback at first but then hugs me back more fiercely than I expected. "I will always be here to protect you Jo. If nothing else, at least require that of me."

I say nothing as we sit there on the couch clinging to each other for entirely different reasons.

"So what ever happened to Ava's sister?" I say, hoping to guide the conversation back to a more comfortable place.

"We found them both with social services right after

it happened. We were able to get her out right before The Order learned of her whereabouts. Her sister wasn't so lucky. The Order placed her sister with a family involved within the organization. They've been doing that with children for many years. Any child that they believe may go through the change, they've placed in adoptive situations so they are able to monitor them more closely. Only the ones with . . . certain potential, though," he says and looks at me knowingly.

"Is that what they did with me?"

"Probably so."

I have to fight off the tears as I ask, "So, where do you think my adoptive parents are?"

"Jo, I really can't say . . . I'm sorry. We can't seem to locate them. We don't know what they might have known. In your case things just aren't adding up. It's strange, everything is just . . . different with you."

"When I was in my room I saw . . . blood. Do you think. . ." I can't even get the words out before looking away.

"I'm so sorry, Jo. We just don't have any answers yet. We're still figuring out what they want with you. What exactly they think you can or should do.

"You're changing as we've all done, but with you we aren't really sure what to expect. I've seen you do things that. . ."

He looks at me then and, gives me a slight smile. "Let's just say you're just as amazing as we had been led to believe you could be.

Amazing, huh. So that's what he thinks.

"Now let's get some sleep before we introduce you to my world."

Later as I'm lying on the soft brown leather of the couch, I just can't shut my thoughts off. I move around, changing my position every few minutes with the hope that if I can get comfortable enough maybe I'll just fall into an abyss of much-needed sleep.

I look over and see Sandy on a chair. His head is slumped forward and he's fast asleep. I guess he's probably been through his share of sleepless nights.

The fire's still burning brightly, so I watch as the flames dance around in no particular pattern. I stare at the huge circle hanging above, the color of its metal taking on an almost amber hue from the reflection of the flames. The movement of the flames brings to life all the symbols that are etched around it. Staring at them, my mind goes blank and I finally begin to shut down.

When I wake up I immediately remember everything. Visions of my parents being held somewhere or even hurt and in pain flash through my mind. I sit up on the couch trying to take deep breaths. Trying to control my mind, my body's reaction. I glance up at the huge metal circle and feel instantly comforted by its presence.

Ava is standing beside the couch.

"Jo, are you all right?"

I can't answer, can't say anything as I just sit there trying to take deep breaths but knowing that my resolve is teetering on the brink. Sensing my potential emotional breakdown or, who knows, maybe just doing the only thing that comes natural to her in desperate situations, she bends down to me and pushes her hand into my chest.

I straightaway feel that familiar vertigo race through me. My eyes close instinctively, and when I open them a second later I'm standing there facing Sandy. He looks shocked and it only takes me a split second to realize why. He's standing in the middle of the bedroom completely nude. Ava has transported me to his room while he's in the process of getting dressed.

I can't seem to pull my eyes away. I drink in the amazing beauty that is his body. His golden, bronzed skin . . . rippling muscles.

Seemingly embarrassed, he grabs a shirt lying on the bed and throws it over his head.

"I was. . . Ava. . . " I stutter.

Coming to my senses, I turn and walk briskly into the bathroom, closing the door behind me. I must have been holding my breath this whole time, because as I lean against the door I exhale deeply, feeling lightheaded. The bathroom's still steamy from his shower. I close my eyes, breathing in deeply, feeling the dampness of the air relax me. I open my eyes, but I can't shake the image of him standing there. I've never seen a naked guy before . . . I mean not in real life, and especially not someone I know.

Rapping softly on the door he says, "Jo, um . . . sorry about that. I didn't know you.. . . I mean. . . I was just getting dressed. Are you. . . " There's a long pause before he continues, "Jo, can you open the door please?"

Why am I so embarrassed? I mean, he's the one that didn't have any clothes on.

Gathering my composure, I turn and slowly open the door. He's standing there fully dressed looking at me oddly. "I'm sorry that happened," he says.

Staring at his chest, trying to avoid looking him in the eye, I say, "When I woke up, my thoughts . . . "

I look up into those blue-gray eyes and see concern reflected back at me. What's happening to me, why am I having this reaction to him? I turn away from him and catch my face in the mirror.

Staring back at me is a face that's almost unrecognizable. A girl with undeniable beauty . . . but as I look deeper into the rich amber pools, I see something foreign just below the surface. A spark of something . . . something that terrifies me, makes me feel nothing but apprehension and distrust. Who is this person staring back at me? I've already seen first-hand what she's capable of. I realize then that if I don't start getting a handle on who—or what—I am, I may forever lose myself . . . the self I want to be.

Sandy comes up right behind me and softly runs his hand down the length of my hair. I feel a shiver run through my body as I stand there staring at our reflections. We are standing too close. He takes a slight step back but not enough.

"Sandy, I want to thank you for being there for me, for being . . . here for me," I whisper.

"Of course," he says searching my face. "I can't explain it, know that we basically just met, but I feel…"

He can't seem to find the words so I take this opportunity to get myself out of what has surprisingly become an uncomfortable situation.

"There's no doubt that I need you, really need you." I say pausing to look at that handsome face, before suddenly knowing. Knowing how I need to feel.

"There's also no doubt that however crazy my life has gotten, how much I'm struggling with everything . . . that I need . . . heck, want more than anything in the world . . . Mark. I love him." There, I said it. I had to.

He just stands there, soaking it in. I see pain shoot through his eyes before the buzzing starts—his phone vibrating on the bathroom counter. Giving me one last look he leans past me and answers it, then turns and walks away.

"Yeah," he says and then begins to pace around the room. "No, when was the last time she checked in?" he says as I watch him walk back and forth. He glances at me and I know then that something is very wrong. "She won't be able to officially report it yet, so we have some time . . . What of Julian's?"

At this statement I start to feel the panic start to creep up. He's talking about Julian, and "she" must be Gio. Something's happened to them.

"No . . . they're staying with me! As long as they're here I can guarantee their safety!" he says, turning his back to me. "Absolutely not. . . "

Whatever he's told on the other end seems to affect him.

"I understand . . . we're on our way," he says in an exasperated tone.

When he hangs up, I hold my breath, waiting to hear what he has to say and hoping that none of my worst fears have been realized.

"Gio never showed up at any of the safe houses last night, and those at The Circle headquarters can't seem to get a hold of her," he says looking at me and seemingly filtering his next words carefully. "Also . . . they can't confirm that Julian ever made it home."

"What do you mean 'can't confirm'? Is he ok? Did they talk to his parents?"

"They've also disappeared. . . "

I try to comprehend what he's telling me. Julian's parents are missing, too? But why? Why would anyone want to hurt them, or Julian for that matter? I'm starting to get the sinking feeling that it has something to do with me.

"Jo, we have to join the others now. I don't know why, but they think you might be able to help them. Also there's one more thing."

I start to tremble as he gives me a knowing look.

"I'm sorry Jo—Mark is missing too."

I can feel myself falling. Falling in a pit of disbelief. A pit of utter despair. The thought that anything could happen to Mark is unconceivable. Whether he loves me or not doesn't matter. Just knowing that he's all right is enough for me. That's all I need. It's all that matters.

I can tell by the set of Sandy's shoulders that he's upset. "We're gonna find him, Jo. I'm going to do everything in my power to make this right for you."

17

—

We've left the plush green woods that had enveloped us in a blanket of seclusion and safety while at Sandy's cabin and now are headed in the direction of another mountain range. As we drive, the terrain becomes more vast. Sandy speeds along and without so much as a flinch takes a right turn onto a dirt road that seems to come out of nowhere all of a sudden. We race down a road that's surrounded by nothing but a desert of shrub brush and cacti.

Ava is sitting in the back seat just staring out the window. Dust flies up on either side of the vehicle. Sandy's staring straight ahead, seemingly lost in thought. The look on his face, set of his jaw, and intensity of his stare makes me start to feel apprehensive about what lies ahead.

I shift in my seat, and this seems to break his concentration. "Jo, this place we're going, these people. . ."

He sighs and looks in the rearview mirror at Ava then over at me. "Jo, you and Ava are . . . special. I mean, different from anyone we've ever come across. There are so many reasons people want to find you both. Because of this you have to be . . . cautious. Some people have your best interests at heart but others don't."

"I trust you," I say giving him a knowing look.

"That's the problem, Jo. Once we get there, I'm afraid things will be out of my hands somewhat. I'm not exactly sure how much control of the situation I'll be able to keep. And that's what worries me."

He just sits there for a moment before continuing, "Just

trust your instincts, and if you have to . . . trust in your abilities. I've seen what you can do. If you must, protect yourself."

At his words I look back at Ava. Our eyes connect and she smiles at me. I realize how afraid I am of what I can do.

We drive on for about another fifteen minutes, and then I start to see what looks to be a cluster of buildings off in the distance. As we get closer, I'm able to make out what seems to be a large edifice made out of adobe with similar smaller structures surrounding it. Along the top of the main building are three bells with a cross positioned right above them. Looks as if it's one of those old abandoned missions that can be found interspersed all around the edge of the mountain ridge.

Coming right up on it now, I see curved archways and massive columns that were probably once quite beautiful but are now pitting and falling to ruins. In front of the massive structure is a dried-up stone fountain with a partially standing statue in the center of it. What once must have been a statue of a man has broken off in enough parts that it's hard to make out exactly what he is supposed to be doing.

Sandy drives past the mission, headed to a low-lying stone building off to the side by a field of yellow wild flowers. As he gets closer, the front of the strange structure suddenly starts to move. A large portion of it begins to lift up off the ground just as a garage door would. As we get closer I see the whole thing is a facade. He drives the car in, and the door then begins to lower behind us. Looking around I realize we are in some sort of garage. It's bigger than it looked from the outside and is filled with many types of vehicles. The one that catches my eye is a huge military-type Hummer that we pull in next to.

The seemingly stone door closes securely behind us with a boom. Sandy cuts off the engine but before opening his door turns toward me and starts to say something, but then stops and looks around the area as if we aren't alone. He sighs, gives a weak smile, and then says, "Let's go."

As I step out dust fills my lungs. I can see a thin layer of dirt lying on almost everything in here. Upon entering we must have stirred it up a bit because tiny particles are floating in the air all around us. I cover my mouth and nose with my hand as I follow Sandy and Ava through a door in the back of the building. Sunlight instantly warms my skin and I breathe in the fresh air as we walk around the back of the building, headed in the direction of the old mission.

The ground cracks under our weight as if rain hasn't touched this spot in years. Living in the city, I always forget how different the terrain is out here. It's always seemed so brutal and uninhabitable to me.

Once we get to the front of the main building, we follow Sandy up a few stairs and into the building. Upon entering through its very large wooden door, we walk into what seems to be a room that hasn't seen a person in years. Old, harsh-looking furniture is laid out sparingly throughout. That same layer of dirt as was in the garage seems to have found its way in here as well. Suddenly a small door in the back of the room begins to open up. I follow them through and then stare in disbelief.

Although the inside walls look original and weathered, the room is full of high-tech, military-grade equipment, corralled in a glass enclosure. As my mind begins to imagine all the different uses that these machines may have, I notice a man standing inside the enclosure staring at us. He doesn't even blink as I stare back at him. He just looks at me with this intense curiosity. That's when I notice two others on the opposite side of the room doing the same thing. I'm beginning to feel like one of those circus sideshow freaks. I look over at Ava and see her smiling at the one man behind the glass. As usual she's eternally optimistic.

We make our way down a narrow hallway off to the right.

"Hi Jo. . . Ava. . . " a voice says from behind us. I stop walking and spin around. Standing there smiling at us is a man dressed in sand-colored fatigues. Around my father's age, he has an accountant look to him, which causes him to seem out of place in the uniform. He steps forward and reaches a hand out to me. "I'm Adrian."

Hesitantly I shake his hand and am surprised by its roughness. He smiles in an assuring way and then turns his attention to Ava. He seems hard to read somehow. He nods toward Sandy and then has us follow him through a door that I hadn't seen until now.

We end up in a modestly decorated room but otherwise its ambiance is welcoming and serene. Adrian motions for Ava and I to take a seat on a tan sofa that's sitting in the center of the room. Sitting down I look over at Sandy and catch him leaning against the wall by the door, arms folded, staring straight at me with a somber look on his face. He quickly looks away from me and toward Adrian.

Still smiling, he glances over at Sandy before continuing, "I hope Sandy has been hospitable." I nod meekly and look over at Sandy, but he's just glowering at Adrian. I get the impression he doesn't like him very much and wonder what's gone on between these two in the past. I can't imagine that Sandy wouldn't like someone unless he has a very good reason.

As he grabs a rustic wooden chair from the corner of the room and brings it over by the sofa, I think how he must be one of the leaders here. He definitely seems like a no-nonsense type of person. Probably not one for small talk, but I guess when you're dealing with all this crazy stuff, there's just no time.

He places the chair right in front of us and sits down. Leaning forward he smiles and stares at us for a moment before saying, "You have no idea how happy I am to have the two of you here finally. Well, you must have many questions for me, so I'll start by telling you a little about myself.

"It's been more years than you would think possible, since I went through my change, and like you I had an adjustment period. Once I learned to control my . . . special characteristics, I went on to incorporate them into my life. After living many successful and seemingly uneventful years, my life changed forever one day when I met my wife, Maria. I fell completely and utterly in love with her and was lucky enough to have her love me back even though I was. . . " He pauses and looks at me with an expression that seems to bore right through my soul into all my insecurities about Mark. Our eyes connect and I realize that he knows. Of course he knows. He must know everything about me if they've been watching me. He must know about Mark, must understand my feelings.

He breaks our connection by turning away before continuing. "After we got married, we had a son. Years later we realized that he was beginning to go through the change himself. He had in fact inherited from me the genetic DNA strand that makes us . . . different. It's not a very common trait to pass along

that's why there have never been many of us, and now, of course . . . there are even fewer." A spark of anger ignites in his eyes for a moment, but just as quickly as it comes, it's gone.

"Around this time an organization called The Order. . . "
Upon hearing this name I glance over at Sandy. Adrian sees me and says, "I'm sure Sandy has filled you both in on them. And I'm sure he told you about their connection to the

murders . . . yes?" He looks strangely at us then.

Ava and I both nod.

"That's what started all this," and he motions to the area around us. "We're just a group of individuals, much like yourself, that formed not only to protect our kind but to find . . . that certain person who we believe has the capability to . . . well, let's just say preserve these characteristics within all of us.

"As you've now undoubtedly figured out, you are this person, Jo."

I can feel a lump in my throat as I ask him.

"How exactly am I supposed to . . . help everyone? I mean, I can't even control these things . . . these episodes when they are happening to me. How am I supposed to be able to. . . "

I just sit there staring at him as my question lingers in the air.

He leans forward in his chair and looks at me. I see a quick look of uncertainty flash in his eyes before he says, "You'll learn to control these abilities better as you finish going through the change. We've all had to get accustomed to it. Your change may be slightly harder, but don't worry . . . we're here to help you. Help you reach your potential, so to speak.

"From what I've heard about you, I have no doubt that you will be able to rise to the occasion."

He seems to get lost in thought for a moment. When he starts again his voice has an edge to it I hadn't noticed before.

"Jo, there's something inside you. Something that has a lot of people spooked and just as many scrambling to find you. To figure out exactly what it is you're capable of and what role you play in all of our lives. Heck, even those at The Order are acting out of character concerning you."

He abruptly stands up and starts to pace about the room. I watch him walk back and forth, deep in thought. "What we do know is around the time of the killings, their intel pointed to a new energy source manifesting itself in one of our kind. The search for that special person began and well, here you are. I mean, it's completely unprecedented," he says smiling at me in disbelief.

"The current energy source is in its pure form, and from what we've been able to gather it's been hidden in this area of the Southwest all this time. Basically since it . . . since we all started this process of changing. And your specific change must be what started affecting it. As our pure source fades, you . . . change."

I can tell he's now thinking out loud as he looks at me. I get the impression he's baffled by the idea of me having some sort of hold over everyone. This young, clueless-looking teenager that's on the verge of tears most of the time and confused the rest. Why me, and if not me . . . what then? Things would have stayed the same? Life would have continued as before without the factions, the war . . . without the killings?

My mind starts to go down a dark road. Blame is beginning to seep in, and all I can think about are the others that have already been killed . . . because I am . . . just because I exist. That's when I start to feel those ever-fragile walls holding in my emotions begin to give a little.

"All this sorrow . . . because of me."

His expression softens as he realizes where I'm going with this.

"No! You had nothing to do with what happened to the others. The decisions made by The Order are theirs and theirs alone. Their fear and greed led them to do the terrible things they did, not you."

Upon hearing these words, a sense of calm starts to creep

into my being once more. I let out a sigh and look over toward Sandy, but he's gone. I didn't notice him leave, and now not having him here makes me feel instantly vulnerable. I look over at Ava, and she's just sitting there looking at her folded hands in her lap. I reach over, take one, and give it a reassuring squeeze.

Misreading my actions and continuing with his train of thought, he says, "I realize you both have been affected . . . affected by this decision to retain the energy for their own selfish needs. You have lost someone close to you, as I have. My son was a casualty to their . . . cause." I can hear the disgust in his voice and the same anger that I witnessed earlier within him is now burning brightly in his eyes. He goes over to a cabinet that's resting in the corner. He pulls something from within it and walks back over and hands it to me.

"This is the head of The Order. Irina Von Hilton." I look down and stare at the picture he's just handed me. It's a headshot of a woman. A strikingly beautiful woman. A woman I can tell is used to being in control. Even in the picture she seems to be in command, to dominate . . . just with her mere manifestation.

"She's the one that's responsible for killing our kind . . . your friend . . . my son," he almost growls. He turns and faces the wall for a moment before sighing, then turning to face us again. Regaining some of his earlier composure he looks right in my eyes. "She's different, like the two of you. Something locked away in her genetic code manifests differently for her then it does for the rest of us. With you, we at least have an inkling of your differences, but with her . . . let's just say we haven't been able to gather all that intel yet.

"I do know that whatever it is that makes her unique is something she's not willing to live without—so for that, I will do everything in my power to take her down, even if that means we must end her!"

And that's when I realize why Sandy doesn't completely trust him. His son's death has left him bent on revenge above all else.

I stare at the picture and think about this woman. How much pain she has caused

how much she is hated. Does she know . . . does she even care? Whatever it is that she is trying to hold on to . . . could it ever be worth all this?

"Adrian."

I look up and see that Sandy is standing there. When did he come back in? Relief washes over me when I see him. I feel safe again.

He motions for Adrian to come with him a moment and they head toward the door. Before they walk out, Sandy glances over at me, and for a brief moment I see something in his eyes that sends shivers up my spine.

What's happened to make him look at me like that? Something bad has happened, I can feel it. Oh no, has something happened to Julian . . . his parents?

I look over at Ava, and there's not a hint of a smile on her face. She looks scared and small when she's not being her usual perky self.

"I'm sure everything's alright," I say and give her a weak smile.

"That lady . . . that Von Hilton lady in the picture probably wants to run tests on me."

"Huh?"

"Gio said something to Sandy about that one time. About how if they ever got their hands on me, they'd probably give me to their scientist people or whatever over there to study. To figure out what makes me different than the rest."

Her eyes start to tear up a little. I guess this Adrian guy

isn't instilling much faith in her. This is probably why Sandy just wanted to keep us at the cabin. She was happy there.

"Don't worry," I say softly. "You're not the only one that's different. I have no intention of ever letting anyone hurt you," I say putting my arm around her. I give her a slight hug and smile before saying, as convincingly as I can, "As you've probably heard, I do have a few tricks up my sleeve."

Even as the words come out of my mouth, even as I try to get her to believe me, I wonder if it's more for her benefit or mine. Maybe I can convince myself I'm the one that can bring hope to a dying, what? Species? Kind? What are we exactly?

18

Sandy bursts through the door, startling me. "I need you both to come with me!" Seeing the look on his face, I respond without question. Ava and I jump up and follow him out of the room. "There are some things happening right now. We're trying to scramble and figure it out, but no matter what, stay with me . . . just stay safe." He looks at me intensely and I can tell he's wanting to take us away from here just as much as he's wanting to enter the door we're in front of. "Don't worry, I'm ready."

He gives me a look that tells me he's anything but reassured and walks through the door. Ava follows him with me right behind.

Upon entering I realize now where most of the people in this organization have been this whole time. It seems to be some sort of main control room. There are about two dozen people here busy doing various tasks, but when we walk in everyone stops and stares at us with that same look of unbridled curiosity as the man we'd first encountered when we came here. But just as quickly, they go back to whatever they were doing before.

In the center of the room is a huge table with many people standing around it. I notice Adrian standing next to a woman that has her eyes locked on me. She's not dressed like all the others here in those desert-themed fatigues. I can only assume it's Maria, but notice she seems quite a bit older than him.

Sandy goes right up to the table as Ava and I stay off

to the side. While the whole room is abuzz with activity, a man is rattling off information to those around the table in the most monotone, devoid-of-any-emotion voice I've ever heard. It's not until I hear Adrian chime in that I start to listen to what is actually being said.

"They have places all over this region. What's so special about this particular location? It's in the middle of the goddam mountains!" Adrian shouts as he slams his hand down on the table.

"Sir, our man believes this might be the pure source. That the other location was a . . . decoy of sorts."

"But all this time. How could we have missed it? I mean, what's changed?" Adrian's frustration is apparent as he runs his hands through his hair. The woman next to him briefly takes her eyes off of me just long enough to whisper something in his ear. Whatever she says causes him to look my way, and then as if on cue he regains his composure and continues questioning the other man.

"So if their board of directors did in fact meet, then what? Why this act of urgency on their part? They've never so much as forgotten to dot an I, cross a T. And now this."

Sandy chimes in before Adrian can say any more. "Do we believe that they know where she . . . we are?"

"No. There hasn't been any indication that we've been compromised. Should that ever happen, we have protocols in place." Adrian glowers at Sandy.

"Adrian, I still can't help but feel that having them here is foolish! Why take the risk?" Sandy asks, raising his voice.

Leaning forward on the table toward Sandy, Adrian sneers, "Granted your intel has been helpful and I've had no reason to question your allegiance until now, but . . . I don't like you! I don't like the fact you aren't a team player. That you have a place, heck . . . a life away from here that we aren't privy to. In my book, that's suspicious no matter how you justify it. You aren't the only one here that's suffered. You act like you can play by your own rules! If I say she stays—she stays!"

"You said it yourself, they're acting desperate . . . out of character! Are you really willing to put her at risk? I mean, you don't even know what's going on with Gio, with. . ." He looks at me then, and I can tell he regrets saying it. My mind immediately goes to Mark. To Julian.

The room is quiet for a moment, and I wonder if these people know more about what's going on then they are owning up to. Is this what Sandy was talking about when he said to trust my instincts? To watch my back. He doesn't completely trust these people, and from what I'm hearing not only do they seem to be a step behind The Order, they don't seem to have my best interests at heart. What exactly is their ultimate agenda?

My thoughts are interrupted as a man comes over from a computer set against the wall across the room. Adrian turns to face him saying something in a low voice. Adrian just stands there, his back to me for a few moments while the man that had spoken to him just stares straight ahead with a look on his face that's void of any emotion.

After a few moments Adrian turns around, and the man walks back over to his station. Adrian says something to the woman next to him, and she gasps and looks at me briefly before whispering something. He nods and turns around. Everyone at the table is silent, staring at him, waiting to hear what he has to say. He glances my way then squares his shoulders and proceeds to tell the room that two more bodies have been found and identified.

"Who did they find?" I ask, dreading the answer with all of my being.

Adrian looks to Sandy and pauses before looking at me and saying more matter-of-factly than I would have thought possible:

"We've found the bodies of your parents."

I stand there for what seems like eternity staring at this man that has just told me that my family has been murdered. That the only two people who have been in my world my entire life, who have loved me unconditionally, are no longer.

I can feel my body reacting but my mind has already shut down. I begin to pant and immediately fall to my knees. Sandy kneels beside me as the glow that's starting to emanate from my chest spreads throughout my body. A moan escapes my lips, and I look over at Sandy and realize he's no longer kneeling. He's sprawled out on the floor beside me, gasping for air. I look around and see that everyone seems to be having the same reaction.

Maria's there then. By my side, yelling something at me . . . shaking me. What does she want? What's happening? I can't focus . . . my thoughts keep jumping around in my head.

My mom's laughing at my dad. His interpretations of movies have always been hilarious. I guess it's his quirky. . .

I'm jolted back by a slap across my face. I see her talking to me . . . saying something, but I can't focus on the words. I feel a slight sting where she hit me. Instinctively I reach up to touch it but stop when I notice my hand. I hold it out and stare at the amber gleam radiating from it.

My thoughts shift again, and I'm picturing the alley behind the movies. I look ahead and see two bodies on the ground. I'm running toward them, trying to get to them, to save them. I'm there then, but it's not my parents I'm staring down at. It's Mark and Julian.

"No!" I scream as I jump up. I see her hand reach for

me again. A slap, a punch . . . not knowing her intentions, I reach out quickly and grab a hold of it. She screams out in pain, startling me, bringing me back to my surroundings.

Maria's in front of me, tears streaming down her face. She glances around the room then and runs over to Adrian. His gasps are starting to smooth out. She kneels beside him and helps him try to sit up, but he's weak. She reaches out to rub his back, but draws her hand away with a gasp. It seems as though she has burned it somehow. She looks my way then in disbelief. Did I burn her?

My senses are back, and I glance around the room at all the people sprawled out on the floor. I see Sandy, and my mind clicks back on completely. Running over, I fall to the ground beside him and listen for his breathing. His breaths are short and raspy, but he's breathing nonetheless. His eyes are open, and he slowly turns his head toward me. Our eyes connect for a brief moment before I remember . . . remember her. Ava.

Looking over to where she was standing unharmed just moments ago, I see her lying on her side. I almost trip on Sandy as I scramble to get to her. I dive toward her, sliding on my knees before I come to a halt right beside her. Her eyes are closed, and I can't see any signs that she's breathing. I turn her so she's resting on her back and put my head on her chest, listening and even feeling for any proof that she's still alive. Nothing.

"Ava!" I almost scream as I shake her shoulders, hoping to somehow rouse her. I look toward Sandy for help and see that he's up on his feet now but still bent over in pain. He stares at me, and with an anguished grunt heads toward us.

I realize I'm crying as I watch my tears leave little damp droplets all over her beautiful but now completely ashen face. He's there then, pushing me aside weakly. First he checks for breathing and then begins to administer CPR. After the third chest compression, the exertion seems to be too much for him and he stops to catch his breath. He gives me a pained look, and I know what I have to do.

Leaning over her I start with the chest compressions again. I had gone over CPR in class last year and had even practiced on the dummy girl they brought in. It's starting to come back to me, but I'm still not sure if what I'm doing is even remotely right. I look over at Sandy, and he stops me and points to her mouth. I tilt her head back and give her my lifesaving breaths, but nothing. She's not responding.

I push on her chest and give her another breath but I'm having trouble now as my emotions are taking hold. Sandy's there again, taking over for me. He seems stronger now and more focused. After checking again for breathing, he gives me a pained look. We can't stop trying.

What have I done? Why is this happening? I'm panting again and feel Sandy reach out to try to calm me down.

I stare down into her angelic face and start to sob. I'm shaking all over as I think about her lifeless body just lying here and within it a heart that is still, not beating. I focus on its image in my mind. If only there was something I could do to get that motionless mound of muscle to jolt back awake. Instinctively I put both my hands on her chest, hoping that somehow I can will her heart to again start pumping life-giving oxygen and blood through her body. I squeeze my eyes shut, and my mind immediately jumps to a lesson I remember having on the anatomy of the heart. How it's basically electrical. It needs to be jumpstarted, to be woken up by a surge of—

Her body convulses under my hands. My eyes fly open, and I yank my hands away as if I'm being burned, although I feel nothing. Sandy leans over her to check for breathing.

He turns toward me and says, "You . . . did it. I saw a flash and then . . . "

Others come and kneel around her.

"She has a steady pulse, but we need to get her to a monitoring station," one man says in a raspy, strained voice. I wonder if I had anything to do with him sounding like that. I'm sure I did, and instantly feel guilty.

As they position themselves around her, I notice that no one seems to be looking at me. Whenever someone gets close enough, they recoil as if just the slightest touch from me could kill them.

I stand up and look around the room. Adrian and the woman that now I'm positive must be Maria, as she wasn't affected by my meltdown, are gone. The few people that are left in the room seem to be still doing various jobs but not with the same gusto as before.

"She'll be all right, thanks to you," Sandy says, coming up beside me.

I take a step away from him, not wanting to touch him in any way just in case my touch could somehow hurt him again.

"If it weren't for me, she wouldn't have almost died to begin with," I say.

Sandy just sighs and stands there beside me. He seems to be choosing his words wisely as everyone should probably start to do from now on anytime they need to communicate with me. I've never felt more like a freak than I do right now.

"Jo," Sandy says, "you're still going through your change. You're not completely able to control . . . things. Your emotions can guide your abilities right now, and your abilities just seem to be more . . . "

"Lethal," I chime in.

"No, well . . . yes, but also more . . . connected . . . Oh

hell, Jo. You definitely have some link to us all, but I know you. You would never hurt anyone intentionally."

"Unless I lose control again . . . "

"Yes, well . . . "

The doors open and Adrian comes in. He and some other operatives surround the table, and it looks like they're going to continue exactly where they had left off as if nothing had happened.

"I want to apologize to you, Jo. Giving you the news that way . . . "

He pauses and a look creeps into his eyes that I've never seen in him before.

Fear.

"Your response was to be expected, but what I didn't anticipate was your reaction and its outcome. I'm the one to blame for that. I . . . we know you are different, and I should remember to respect that."

I glance over at Maria, and whereas before she couldn't take her eyes off of me, she's now avoiding me all together. I see that her hand is bandaged and my resolve weakens.

"Have you heard anything from Gio?" Sandy asks, getting everyone back on track and breaking this uncomfortable tension.

"No, not yet. If she has been taken to The Order, we expect to hear about it soon. Our contact there will inform us, that is if we don't hear from her directly. But for now we need to determine The Order's sudden interest in this remote mountain location. We've sent some scouts out to check and see if in fact that is the location of the pure source."

Sick of feeling as though I only know half of what's going on, and figuring since I'm such an important part of all this, I step forward and direct a question at Adrian. "What do you mean by pure source?"

"I haven't explained everything to her yet. I figured she had a lot to digest already," Sandy says more matter-of-factly than apologetically.

Adrian gives him a look that tells me he's probably a little unsure now how much I can take before I combust altogether and take everyone with me. Sandy brushes his concerns away by his tone as he answers my question.

"Remember the energy source I was telling you about that gives us our abilities? Our way of life? The energy that causes you to sometimes feel stronger than normal, almost powerful, if you will?"

I nod at him, thinking especially of the times when I've been running and my body feels so different. Exactly how he describes it . . . powerful.

"I know this is going to sound crazy, but the pure source is a meteorite."

"A meteorite, like from outer space?" I ask almost in disbelief.

"I know what you're thinking, but there actually is scientific evidence that suggests that someone's DNA sequence can be changed or mutated when it comes into contact with high levels of electromagnetic radiation. With us, these mutations in our DNA cause us to change when hormones are produced during puberty. This pure energy source, or meteorite, has been fueling the effects that are caused by the mutations. Take the energy away, and we aren't sure what will happen to us."

Adrian snorts. "Well, I know one person who wouldn't be happy with the outcome, no matter what happened. Von Hilton's made it her mission to see that the energy source never wanes, no matter what the price."

I think then of the woman in the picture. I think of all those she's hurt for her own selfish needs. She must be stopped, and I'm suddenly feeling more up to the task. My parents flash in my mind. Thoughts of revenge, of punishing . . . inflicting extreme amounts of pain to those involved. I'm relating to Adrian more every minute.

"So this is how the pure source is connected to us all, but especially to you, Jo."

Everyone's silent. It's as if they are all holding their breaths at the thought that I'm somehow directly connected to this source, and the hold I have over all of them.

"But a meteorite? Are you sure?"

"Yes, we're sure. Certain meteorites contained building blocks of DNA. This DNA has obviously been formed extra-terrestrially. The Order wants to understand its structure. They have their best scientists working on it.

Images flash in my mind of men and women in lab coats working around the clock trying to piece together the clues that make up this meteor that's fallen from space and its con-nection with us. Hovering over data and examining pieces of rock.

"So we know the board members are acting out of charac-ter, scrambling, making mistakes . . . but why?" Adrian says and looks down at the table.

"Jo . . . you ok?" Sandy asks with nothing but concern in his voice.

I realize I must have zoned out, lost in my own dark thoughts. My minds sharpens and I look around the room, quickly hoping that I haven't caused any problems. Everyone seems fine, just a little unsure and probably worried for their own safety.

Adrian hesitantly chimes in. "Jo, maybe you should go lie down. You've had a lot of things thrown at you and—"

"No!" I shout, surprising even myself but knowing that leaving is the last thing I could ever do right now.

I sigh and gather my thoughts before continuing in a more controlled manner. "I'm sorry I've allowed my emotions to get the best of me. I can do better."

I look around the room, attempting to make eye contact with everyone one by one before finally letting my gaze rest on Sandy.

"I understand that I have to moderate my thoughts better, to . . . stay in control. I know this now, and I'm sorry but you can't get rid of me. This is my fight, too."

I push the images of my parents to the back of my mind. To that place that I've been shoving things for now, knowing that somewhere down the line this is exactly the place I'm going to go to when the time is right.

With my thoughts and emotions surprisingly in check, I continue. "They've hurt so many people, innocent people, people like us. You brought me here to help you, and that's what I want to do."

Adrian stares at me, and for the first time since I've met him, he seems . . . hopeful.

"Jo, as you're aware, the energy manifests more powerfully in a few of our kind, like it has with you and Ava. We believe this may be a common factor among some members of The Order."

"That doesn't make what they're doing right."

"Of course not, but if you had the ability to, say, live forever, well . . . let's just say that could change the way you thinks about the energy source."

"Are you telling me this energy gives them immortality?"

"We all heal more quickly and age much slower than those without abilities, but we've learned that these particular five members of this board may in fact manifest the energy for eternal youth. The evidence isn't conclusive, but preliminary findings suggest this to be true."

"But how, how is that even possible?"

"Something to do with the energy slowing cellular aging—and in their case halting it altogether."

I think about the fact that these people may never die, that they'll continue to kill just to keep themselves alive. Perhaps, but although their bodies are preserved, their souls have long since died. I can picture them . . . scheming, conniving . . . coming up with different ways to keep their hearts pumping, blood flowing . . .

"As you know, the best way to kill our kind is to cause our internal energy source to spontaneously combust. That's what this is for. . . "

He throws on the table the Taser-type device. Haunting images of that poor girl in the alley flood my thoughts. I stare at this piece of machinery and wonder how anyone could ever even think up such a horrible mechanism.

"This is their creation and has always been their weapon of choice. Get in quick, put someone's lights out . . . literally . . . then leave. It leaves someone completely burned from the inside out, so an autopsy is pretty much useless."

Speaking to me Sandy says, "I know they must want to get their hands on you, Jo. They're afraid of you—of what you represent. We have no way of knowing for sure what they would attempt to do to you. They may actually think killing you could restore the energy back to the pure source. You're connected somehow, everyone knows that . . . but what nobody knows is how. If there's one thing I've learned about The Order, they always seem to be one step ahead of us. Help us if you must, but please, Jo, be careful. I do believe your survival is crucial."

19

—

The ball flies through the air and effortlessly enters the basket with a whoosh. I look over at him, and he flashes me one of his cocky grins. Beautiful brown eyes twinkle, and he comes over to wrap his arms around me. I feel so happy right now, which is strange given my surroundings.

Alarms are blaring. People seem frantic . . . chaotic. The basketball court is gone and so is Mark. I look around, trying to collect my thoughts. Where was I? Is my mind playing tricks on me? I realize then I was hallucinating. What the hell is wrong with me?

"Jo. . ."

I see Sandy's face, and I find myself nodding as my eyes follow him out of the room. Where's he going . . . Ava . . . oh right. He said Ava.

Those alarms are starting to really get on my nerves. I walk over to one of the security screens in the room and stare at it in disbelief. They're here . . . they are actually here.

Black SWAT-team uniforms swarm the mission grounds.

I'm frozen in front of the screen as I watch the fighting begin. A few men in desert fatigues that I never even noticed coming in here are attempting to defend us.

As I watch the screen the alarms blare on. Almost everyone has left the room. I can't move. I seem to be rooted to this spot. Am I waiting for something? My mind shifts through the last few minutes. I can't shake this odd feeling I have. I just can't . . . and so I look back at the security screen.

The black uniformed figures begin to enter the mission

as the bodies of those men that were just a moment ago alive are now lying on the ground, smoke rising from each.

"It's all right, honey."

I spin around, and my dad is standing there smiling at me. He reaches out and strokes my hair. "Don't worry Josie, everything is going to be just fine."

I'm instantly relieved and comforted to see him. As we stand there staring at each other, I really do feel like everything will be all right.

"Jo, we need to get you out of here."

"Everything will be all right," I say.

"What . . . no, Jo . . . we need . . . what's wrong with you?"

Adrian is standing in front of me. Am I losing my mind or is this all part of that stupid change I'm supposed to be going through?

"Jo, what's going on? Are you ok?"

Just then the most booming voice I've ever heard resounds through the room.

"Step away from her!"

I turn around, and it takes me a minute to take it all in. I can see everything that's going on in the room, but my mind is trying to play catch up.

They're fast. I mean so fast all I make out for that split second is movement . . . black movement. I look down and see Adrian lying in a heap at my feet. Someone grabs my arm, but before I can yank it away I hear, in that same voice as before, "Let her go!" The grip from my arm is instantly released, and the man dressed in one of those intimidating black uniforms takes a step away from me.

How did this happen? Only minutes ago we were coming up with a plan. I was proclaiming my ability to help these people. I'm a fool to think that I could ever be anything but a frightened teenage girl.

My eyes are drawn to a scuffle over to the right. I stare, shocked, as another one of these intruders shoves a man to the ground and then goes on to extinguish him with one of those horrible Taser devices. I look away, but the rank stench of burning flesh makes my stomach roil. I can't help but glance back over and immediately regret it. Another image of death forever embedded in my mind.

"Adrian!"

I look toward the door just in time to see one of the men grab Maria as she tries to run past them to get to Adrian. She struggles to get away, but her determination seems to be no match for his iron grip.

"What did you do to him?" she asks in a voice trembling with emotion.

A mountain of a man looms from a corner in the room and walks over to her. How did I not notice him before now? As he stops right in front of the two of them, he predominates. I stare in awe at his massive frame but fear that it's not his size that fills me with such dread.

"You must be Maria," he growls at her, causing her to stop struggling.

"My . . . husband . . . what did you. . . ." she asks breathlessly.

"Your husband will be coming with me. I believe he has very valuable information to share that my superiors deem crucial. That is, unless you yourself can give me the name of the mole. . ."

"I don't know what you're—"

Before she's even able to complete her sentence he whips out a gun and shoots her in the head. Her body instantly goes limp and the man who seconds before had a grip on her lets go, and she falls to the ground with a thud.

I stand there horror stricken.

"Get him out of here!"

Two men scramble and carry Adrian out of the room. That's when the monster of a man looks my way. With eyes devoid of any emotion he stands there for a moment just staring at me, intimidating me with every second that passes.

He smirks before saying, "So you're the little girl that everyone's getting such a hard-on about."

He starts to slowly walk toward me, and I can feel myself begin to shake ever so slightly. My mouth fills with saliva as fear seeps out of my every pore. He stops and takes a deep breath as if he could actually smell it.

"I believe you're done here!" a voice says from the door.

It's Julian.

I can't believe my eyes. How is it that he's here . . . in this place . . . now?

"You've gotten who you came for," Julian says in a surprisingly authoritative tone.

"Not everyone. . . " the man says, still staring down at me in such a cold, calculated way that I can't tell if he wants to murder me or eat me.

"You know what will happen if you lay one finger on her, Mitchell," Julian says and steps closer.

This finally seems to break his concentration.

"Ok, mama's boy. I'll give you a chance to do it your way before I step in and do it mine. . . "

As Julian comes closer to me, my first instinct is to run over and throw my arms around him, but I can't . . . I don't. I'm so confused. The alarms that just minutes before were blaring throughout the building have been silenced, but for me they haven't stopped.

Julian comes up, wrapping his arms around me. He holds me tighter than I would have ever wanted him to and whispers in my ear, "Jo ... you have no idea how long I've waited for this moment." I feel the intensity of his embrace, and my mind scrambles to try to make sense of it all.

"We can finally be together . . . really together."

Starting to feel really freaked out, I push away from him.

"Julian, what's going on? How did you get here? Where's Mark . . . Gio?"

The other man snorts, and I realize he's now standing against the wall watching our entire interaction with amused disdain.

Ignoring him, Julian takes my hand in his, and with a perplexing amount of affection says, "Jo, I know you're confused. You have a ton of questions, and I'm going to fill you in on everything, trust me. But right now, it's important that you come with me. We have to get you safe."

"Going with him will not make you safe."

I look over and see Sandy standing at the door with a gun pointed at Julian. He slowly walks through the room, and before I can let out a warning there's a crack as Mitchell knocks him down with a backhanded punch to his face.

"Sandy!" I hear myself yell. I start to run over to him, but Julian grabs my arm.

Ava appears, kneeling beside Sandy. Where did she come from? I try to wrangle free from Julian's grasp, but he's not letting me. "Julian, let me go . . . what are you doing?"

"Protecting you, Jo, just like I always have. . . "

"He's with them. . . " I hear a raspy voice say and look over at Sandy. He's sitting up with Ava's help, blood running from his nose into his mouth. Mitchell is standing over both of them with a gun aimed and ready.

Flashing back to Maria, I feel my heart rate increase as I yell, "No! . . . Don't!"

I see Mitchell gulp, and a sheen of sweat breaks out over his brow, but he doesn't lose his focus. I can feel Julian's grip loosen ever so slightly.

"Jo." I hear Sandy say in that same raspy voice, but this time it seems a little more strained than before. "Calm down, Jo. Just breathe . . . you . . . have to take control . . . "

It's happening again. I look over at Ava's contorted face and close my eyes, taking deep breaths. It's going to be all right . . . it's all going to be all right. I keep telling myself this until I can feel my internal sensors are calming down.

Opening my eyes, I see Sandy give me a weak smile. Mitchell still has his gun pointed at him but quickly glances my way, and I see the uncertainty in his eyes.

I remember then what Sandy said and look up at Julian. I don't know if it's the question he sees in my eyes or the fact that my emotionally driven connection to him caused him to momentarily lose a significant amount of oxygen but he lets go of my arm.

"Julian, are you . . . with. . . "

I can't even bring myself to ask. Tears sting my eyes at the thought.

I think back on him and Sahara in the parking lot. On the many times throughout the last few months that he's acted so strange . . . so different. But no, he was taken. Taken along with Gio and Mark . . .

I mean, his parents are missing . . . aren't they?

I'm frantically trying to piece the clues together.

"Jo . . . whatever you're thinking right now . . . you have to understand. I've never done anything but protect you. Protect you from those who don't understand you, understand what you represent, understand who you are. Who you are to me."

It's getting hot in here. I look down at my hands and see that they're trembling. Julian can't be involved, he just can't be.

"Sahara wanted to kill you so many times."

The mention of her name causes my senses to sharpen.

"She was a hothead, yeah, but not dumb enough to go against me . . . to hurt you," he says, and I see a flash of anger in his eyes before he looks away.My mind's reeling . . . that night at the fair . . . in my dad's Jeep. All these images are running through my head. Not hurt me . . . how can he say that? She was a monster and he knew it, but still allowed me to go on . . . in the dark, unprepared. Protecting me? Could that actually be what he was doing?

Having regained all of his earlier eloquent composure, Mitchell says, "Yeah mama's boy, you're a real big tough guy, aren't you?"

Julian shoots him a look and Mitchell only smirks.

That's when Sandy says, "You're her son, aren't you? We knew she had one, but . . . "

Ignoring him, Julian looks back at me.

"Jo, you don't have all the facts. I know you're confused right now. Come with me and I'll explain everything. Everything. You'll be safe, I promise. I can keep you safe . . . I would never let anything happen to you. I couldn't . . . I love you too much. You have to trust me, Jo . . . please."

The look on his face is so sincere that I can't do anything but believe every word he says. But how can I? He's kept so much from me. He hasn't been truthful. Would he really start now?

"Jo," Sandy says in a clear voice. "He's Irina Von Hilton's son. The leader of The Order. Son of the one person that's hurt you the most. My god, Jo . . . do you really think he has anyone's best interests at heart other than. . . "

"Shut it!" Julian yells and walks over and kicks Sandy in the face. The action is so violent, so matter-of-fact. Julian's face is contorted with rage when he turns back to face me. All I can do is stand there in shock, unable to move . . .

Ava falls to Sandy's side just as Mitchell makes a call on his radio.

I've never seen Julian look like this before.

"Yes! So Irina Von Hilton's my mother, but that has nothing to do with you and I! Damn it, Jo, all I've ever done is love you. I mean hell, I stood by you, watched while you dealt with your feelings for those other guys. I mean . . . Aiden! Really, Jo, Aiden? Mark at least I kind of got . . . you'd had a thing for him for so long. I was willing to stand on the sidelines while you got that out of your system . . . but Aiden! Hell no! I wasn't about wait around for that loser to . . ."

"Julian, what are you talking about? Aiden was your friend."

My heart's pounding, and I can't understand why he's saying these things. I know we're in an impossible situation right now. I know he's angry, but. . .

"My friend, Jo? Come on. He was just an obstacle . . . an obstacle between us. Don't you see that? You didn't see it then, but don't you see that now? Jo?"

I can feel myself getting queasy. What is he telling me?

"Julian . . . are you saying you had something to do with Aiden's death?"

I hear the words come out of my mouth but my mind can't grasp them.

"Ok, pansy, we're gonna do this my way," Mitchell says, pointing his gun at Julian. "My orders were to bring them both in, and although your mama has faith in you, I see you for the waste of space you are."

Turning his attention to me, he says, "Everyone's so goddam scared of what you can do, but just try your shit on me, and I'll hit you were it goddam hurts the most."

I have no idea what he's talking about until two of men show up at the door. As I look past them, I realize then what he means.

That's when my heart sinks.

20

M ark tries to run past the two men in front of him to get to me, but one of them grabs him, and he doubles over from a punch to the gut. He falls to his knees with a grunt.

"No!" I yell, starting in his direction, but Julian stops me.

Mitchell points his gun at Mark's head.

"Ok, bitch, I'm gonna make this as plain as I can. You come with me, or I put a bullet in his head!"

"Mitchell, what the hell, you brought him here?" Julian asks incredulously.

All this time I had been pushing away any thoughts of Mark, and as I see him here, I realize that a part of me had actually feared the unthinkable. "I'll go with you, just don't hurt him!" I say without hesitation.

"No, Jo," Mark says doubled over.

"Julian . . . he killed your parents. He tricked Gio . . . we. . . "

The man to his right smashes his fist into Mark's jaw, sending him sprawling.

I just stare. My mind and body seemingly frozen in shock as I just stand there and stare at Mark lying on the floor, attempting to get up on all fours.

Julian steps forward. "Jo, I had no choice. We discovered your parents . . . could no longer be trusted. We couldn't take the risk, I wouldn't . . . not with you."

I can hear the fear in his voice.

He wants to explain his actions, to make me understand. He's afraid. But afraid of what? Is he afraid I'll hurt him, or worse . . . hate him?

Do I?

I just stand there looking at him trying to explain, feeling the heat begin.

I hear his words but don't understand them. I can't.

"Enough of this shit! You," Mitchell says, pointing at one of the men who came in with Mark. "Grab her and let's get the hell out of here!"

I feel the hand grab my arm and pull me. The next thing I know, I'm in his arms. Mark has managed to stand up and to somehow get a hold of me before they lead me out of the room.

I can feel the steady rhythm of his heartbeat against my body. I breathe in his scent as he whispers to me, "I love you."

Grunting, he falls down at my feet as Julian stands there, knuckles white, clasping a steel blade in his hand.

For a second there's something in his eyes . . . regret, maybe. The next second it's gone, replaced by pure rage.

"One day you'll realize I'm the only one who loves you! Loves you for who you really are!" he spits at me with his jaw clenched.

"Jo!"

Ava's right beside me, kneeling by Mark. She's touching him, checking for a pulse. She looks up at me, and the look on her face sends a jolt through my body.

I'm instantly on fire . . .

"You stupid son of a bitch!" Mitchell says, hitting Julian across the face with his gun, sending him flying.

My insides feel like they're burning. A hollow pit, completely on fire . . . threatening to completely combust. My breaths are coming as shallow gasps. Burning . . . I'm burning . . .

Ava looks back at Mark and shoves her hands against his chest.

He's gone . . .

I stand there burning . . . staring at the spot were, just a second before, Mark had lain.

It happens then. I watch as Ava falls to her side, gasping for air.

Falling to my knees, I'm unable to keep my balance as the faces of all those I love—all those I've lost—run through my mind.

The pain is almost unbearable.

My heart's breaking and it hurts so much . . . so very much that it's hard to breathe.

"Oh my god, Jo!"

Julian's kneeling in front of me now with a look of horror on his face.

"What the hell did you do!" he shouts at Mitchell.

"Saved your ass! Relax, she'll heal."

Looking down I see it then, blood. Blood soaking through my shirt.

"Grab her and let's get the hell out of here!" Mitchell yells to the two men by the door who seem to be trying to gather their strength.

Julian helps them pick me up, and as I'm being carried out, I see her. She's lying on her side with her back to me. Unmoving, her beautiful blond hair is splayed on the floor around her head. As they carry me out of the room and I lose consciousness, her image is all I see.

My eyes fly open and I feel it. The pain that has nothing to do with my wound. My breathing has become a chore that I don't do willingly but instinctively. If it were up to me, I would end it here and now, but my ever-changing body seems to have other plans. This internal fire is almost unbearable.

My captors suddenly cry out in pain and drop me.

"Sir, she's . . . hot!"

"What?"

Hitting the hard floor jolts my senses. My body wills itself up, and I quickly take in my surroundings. I'm still in one of the halls of the mission. Mitchell and his two cronies are looking at me with a mixture of surprise and fear. I'm sure they're wondering what the freak show is going to do next. Well . . . why keep them guessing?

I send a burst of something, energy, heat, I don't know—something—out of my hand and through the abdomen of the first man. Expressionless he slumps over, falling on his side to the floor.

It's the gasp from the other man that draws my attention. Wide eyed, seemingly frozen in fear, he's just standing there looking between me and the man on the floor with the hole where his stomach had been.

I react again and he is instantly delivered the same fate.

That's when I look around the corridor, but Mitchell is gone. I see a door toward the end of the long hall still ajar and head in its direction. I only have two things on my mind as I push through the door.

Julian and Mitchell.

The hot air hits me immediately. I've ended up outside, in the front of the mission. My body begins to yearn. Yearn for the mountain ridge before me. All my instincts are telling me to run. Run for the mountains as fast as I can. Run and don't stop until I get to them. But, get to what?

Fighting hard, I push these feelings away and try to focus

on my objective. That's when I hear someone approaching from behind. I turn around. It's Julian.

He runs right up to me, taking me in his arms. What's he doing? Shoving him away from me, I take a step back and just look at him. All I can do is stare at him, searching. But what am I searching for exactly? Answers? Any recognition of the person that I thought I knew? Even though I want more than anything to punish him for everything he's done, can I? Could I ever bring myself to hurt him?

I realize that's what I want, that's what I need. A reason not to hurt him.

"Jo, don't you see, we can be together now."

"Together? After everything you've done?"

"Everything I've done, I've done for you! Don't you see that?"

"You've destroyed my life!"

"I told you, Jo. I love you."

"No, Julian. If you loved me, you could never. . . "

I'm unable to even finish saying it. My heart's broken and I feel so lost, so confused.

"Do what, Jo? Protect you?"

"Protect me from what! From Aiden . . . my parents?"

I'm beginning to shake uncontrollably. It's taking all the restraint I can muster not to react to the rage building within me.

Push it down . . . buy more time.

I bend over and take a deep breath. Closing my eyes I still feel it. Somewhere, lost in my impending episode, is that yearning, the yearning that has taken hold. I realize now the mountains are looming in my subconscious. Noticing my apparent physical reaction, his demeanor softens and he steps toward me.

"The others wouldn't have understood, couldn't have. I

was only trying to protect you, if not from them then from yourself. In the end I'm the only one that would have really accepted you. I mean, do you honestly believe you and Mark would what . . . marry, have kids? You saw how he looked at you when you killed Sahara. When he saw what you were capable of. You think over time he would just forget about what you really are?"

"I know I'm different! Hell Julian, Mark knew . . . and he loved me anyway!"

"For how long, Jo? What happens when the novelty wears out, huh? When you're just this girl with issues that, let's face it, Jo, aren't exactly your run-of-the-mill problems."

Falling to my knees the tears start to flow down my cheeks as the truth of his words cut like daggers.

"He would have just hurt you in the end, like the others. See, Jo, I know what you are, and I accept you, love you even. My mom . . . she also wants. . . "

The mention of his mother brings me back.

"Your mother! Your mother is a murderer and so are you!"

"Goddamn it, Jo—for you! Aiden didn't matter! And your parents, give me a break . . . they were planted there to watch you. And I have to say, they were doing a pretty shitty job."

As the darkness threatens to take over, I feel that part of me that would find killing him inconceivable try to rise to the surface.

The darkness wins out.

I stand abruptly, squaring my shoulders and halting his movements with just a look. He immediately understands my intentions.

"Jo, wait. . . "

With that I'm thrown back with such a force my head

crashes against the side of the fountain's stones. I lay there stunned for a moment, feeling that gnawing desire begin to make itself known again.

Reaching up I touch the back of my head where the throb has started. I see the light smear of blood on my fingertips, but it's the ebbing glow of my palm that draws my attention. Although part of me cannot seem to comprehend what I've done, another part of me is anything but remorseful.

It's stronger now . . . the yearning. The mountain's beckoning is becoming increasingly overwhelming.

Pushing it away one last time, I head over to him. I know that what I'm about to see will forever change me, but I realize that I must.

He's there on the ground, well . . . at least most of him. I can only bring myself to look at his face. That seems to be the only part of him still completely intact. Bending down, a sob escapes me as I think back to earlier and much better times.

"Oh Julian . . . why did everything have to end up like this?" I whisper to his corpse. I retch right before the sobs begin.

The faces of those I will forever love flash through my mind. It's still impossible to imagine my life without them. I stand up as I suddenly remember. Reaching into my pocket, I pull out the picture I was given earlier.

She's there staring back at me, the woman responsible for everything. I feel it then, the yearning . . . This time, though, I welcome it.

I take off in the direction of the mountains. The pain in my head is starting to subside a bit, but I know, at this moment, that my mental anguish is just beginning.

With my life irreparably changed forever, I know that whatever choices I make or events that are to take place are of no consequence to me. As I've become too aware, my life is not my own. Moving forward, I have but one thing to keep me going.

Revenge.

Epilogue

—

Weston General Hospital

The nurse sees the doctor coming out of an exam room and hurries to catch up with him. It plays back through her mind what a commotion there had been when they found the first guy. Now someone else, and in the same spot.

"Doctor, they found another one!"

Looking up from his notes, the doctor stares at the nurse standing before him, wide eyed and waiting. Waiting for his instructions on what to do next, or maybe just reassurance that this was in fact highly irregular.

"Where is the patient now?"

"They took him into the ER. He's listed as critical, much worse than the first one."

All the nurses had been going on about that first guy ever since he was found. Although much less about his health and more about his looks. So typical, she thinks.

"Do we have any idea who he is?"

"Some star basketball player from a high school around here."

"Found in the same spot, you say?"

"Yeah, it's strange. Almost like someone just put them there, but I don't see how. Staff surely would have seen someone coming or going."

"Well, regardless of how they got here, they're in our

hands now. You go ahead, I'll be there in minute."

The doctor watches as the nurse heads toward the ER. Taking the phone out of his pocket, he glances around briefly before dialing the number.

"I need you to get a message to her," he says to someone on the other end. "Tell her the girl did send them both here. I'm dealing with them now and will continue as instructed once they are recovered."

He then hangs up the phone and heads to the ER, shackled by dread. If he wants to survive this, he knows that nothing better happen to these two.

Discover more books at

dburgardbooks.com